Cal's eyes pinn

They looked so al
warmth through Alex's body.

He had such striking looks, she imagined insecure guys had trouble being around him for fear of not measuring up. "I think he was surprised you had Sergei with you."

"For some people, a dog can be intimidating."

"Surely not when he's with a federal park ranger like you! The boys have let me know they feel safer knowing you take him everywhere."

"Does that go for you, too?"

"I've always felt safe around you."

Even in the dark, his white smile was visible.

When he smiled like that, she had trouble concentrating.

Dear Reader,

Below are the words of Scottish-born American naturalist and explorer John Muir, from his book *The Yosemite*, written in 1912. They make me cry every time I read them.

"No temple made with hands can compare with Yosemite. Every rock glows with life. Some lean back in majestic repose; others, absolutely sheer for thousands of feet, give welcome to storms and calms. Awful in stern, immovable majesty, how softly these rocks are adorned; their feet among beautiful groves and meadows, their brows in the sky, a thousand flowers leaning confidingly against them, bathed in floods of water, floods of light, while the snow and waterfalls, the winds and avalanches and clouds shine and sing and wreathe about them as the years go by, and myriads of small winged creatures—birds, bees, butterflies—give glad animation and help to make all the air into music. It's as if into this one mountain mansion Nature had gathered her choicest treasures, to draw her lovers into close and confiding communion with her."

In my four books set in Yosemite National Park, four noble park rangers and the women they love form a close-knit community to guard her wonders for the next generations. Come on a journey with me in *The Chief Ranger*, *The Ranger's Secret*, *The Bachelor Ranger* and *Ranger Daddy*. Laugh with their precious children, Nicky, Roberta and Ashley, thrill to the secrets uncovered by the Zuni teenage volunteers, learn from the wisdom of Paiute chief Sam Dick. And last but not least, meet Sergei, the brave Karelian Bear Dog, who captures everyone's heart.

Enjoy!

Rebecca Winters

The Bachelor Ranger

REBECCA WINTERS

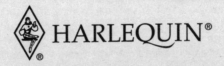

HARLEQUIN®

TORONTO • NEW YORK • LONDON
AMSTERDAM • PARIS • SYDNEY • HAMBURG
STOCKHOLM • ATHENS • TOKYO • MILAN • MADRID
PRAGUE • WARSAW • BUDAPEST • AUCKLAND

Recycling programs
for this product may
not exist in your area.

ISBN-13: 978-0-373-75343-7

THE BACHELOR RANGER

Copyright © 2011 by Rebecca Winters

This edition published by arrangement with Harlequin Books S.A.

For questions and comments about the quality of this book please contact us at Customer_eCare@Harlequin.ca

® and TM are trademarks of the publisher. Trademarks indicated with ® are registered in the United States Patent and Trademark Office, the Canadian Trade Marks Office and in other countries.

www.eHarlequin.com

Printed in U.S.A.

ABOUT THE AUTHOR

Rebecca Winters, whose family of four children has now swelled to include five beautiful grandchildren, lives in Salt Lake City, Utah, in the land of the Rocky Mountains. With canyons and high alpine meadows full of wildflowers, she never runs out of places to explore. They, plus her favorite vacation spots in Europe, often end up as backgrounds for her romance novels, because writing is her passion, along with her family and church. Rebecca loves to hear from readers. If you wish to email her, please visit her website at www.cleanromances.com.

Books by Rebecca Winters

Chapter One

Alex Harcourt poked her head inside the uncluttered office at Hearth and Home, the business her mother had established years earlier. "Bye, Mom. I've made those phones calls and now I'm off for an appointment with the tribal council."

Her mother's blond head lifted. "Maybe you'll be given good news this time."

"I hope so."

As she turned away, the last thing she always noticed was the large framed photograph of six imposing Zuni chiefs taken in 1882. It hung on the wall behind her mother's desk. When Alex was a little girl, she'd play in here and study the picture while her busy mom conducted business with Zuni leaders.

The photo was a print of the original. Her mother explained that these chiefs had gone to Boston to perform ceremonies by the Atlantic Ocean and replenish their supply of sacred seawater. As she grew older, Alex thought a lot about this and wondered why they hadn't traveled to the Pacific Ocean, which was a lot closer to New Mexico.

Over the years she'd received answers to that and

hundreds of other questions. At twenty-six, Alex now realized her love for the Zuni people went as deep as her mother's.

An heiress at thirty through her Trent ancestry, Muriel Trent Harcourt helped orphaned Zuni children to be raised on Trent property in their own ranch houses. Zuni parents without children would become their parents for life. Together they'd have a hearth and home of their own that was paid for by the Trent Foundation.

Alex admired her mother more than anyone in the world and worked for her whenever she could. She felt incredible pride that her mom made it possible for hundreds of Zuni children to remain with their siblings and belong to a real family. At least for these children, there'd be no foster care.

Over the last year Alex had come up with an idea of her own to help the kids and was holding her breath that this meeting would be the first step in achieving that goal.

After leaving Albuquerque, she headed for the Zuni pueblo located one hundred and fifty miles west of the city. Two and a half hours later she parked around the back of the tribal office. Quickly she climbed out of the cream-colored minivan with its green Hearth and Home logo and walked the short distance before knocking on the door.

"Come in."

She stepped inside the council office where she'd sat many times over the years with her mother. Two of the women who made up part of the council smiled at her. One by one the room filled with board members, who ran programs and directed policy. Everyone gathered around the table.

Lonan, a childhood friend four years older than Alex, nodded to her. He had a lot of influence with the Lt. Governor of the Zuni tribe, who came in last and sat down.

"How are you, Alex?"

"I'm fine, Halian. And you?"

"I'm good. We've talked about your proposal. Some still have questions."

"Of course. Ask me anything you want." The council and board members had been asking questions for three months. If they didn't make up their minds soon, her proposal would miss the deadline. She wanted them to say yes so badly she could taste it. But this was only the first step.

When and if she got the go-ahead from the council, she then needed to obtain the approval of the Chief Ranger at Yosemite National Park in California. Alex had nothing but admiration for Chief Vance Rossiter, whose love for the Native Americans led her to believe he'd be totally open to her idea to bring a group of Zuni youth volunteers to the park.

Until his retirement from the U.S. Senate, her father, John Harcourt, had been the senate committee chairman over the federal parks. He'd made many visits to Yosemite during his seven terms of office, often taking Alex with him once she was old enough. It put him in contact with Bill Telford, the current superintendent of the park. Alex had talked with him on many occasions and knew Telford was pushing for more minority groups to be involved. But there were still a lot of ifs in the process.

Halian nodded to each member, allowing them to speak.

"The boys will need one of the tribe to accompany them."

"That's right," Alex agreed. "Do you have someone in mind?"

"I'll go," Lonan volunteered.

Bless you, Lonan. He'd grown up in a Hearth and Home family, one of her mother's favorites. At thirty years, he was a respected member of the council as well as Alex's good friend. If he were willing to accompany the kids, that would hold a lot of weight with the tribe. Lonan was a natural leader, and the boys would work well under him.

Another member spoke up. "What if the families want to talk to their children while they're gone?"

"All the boys and their families with be supplied with cell phones," Alex said. "I'll have a phone so they can call me if they have concerns."

"Eight weeks sounds like a long time," Mankanita commented. "Don't you think so, too?"

Alex heard a plaintive tone in her voice. She and Lonan planned to be married before the year was out. "Eight weeks is the normal period for all volunteers working at the park, but since this will be an experiment, we'll suggest four weeks to start, pending the chief ranger's approval. At that time the boys will talk to their families and vote whether they want to stay another four.

"Remember, this will be a vacation for them, too. Like

all the other volunteers helping to restore the trails, they can spend their time off enjoying everything Yosemite has to offer."

When there were no more questions, she turned to Halian. "The money from the Trent trust fund will pay for clothing and necessities, including the boys' and Lonan's salaries," she assured him. Though they would be volunteers at the park, they still needed to be given a salary to compensate for the paying jobs they wouldn't be doing at the pueblo. "I'll be with them the entire time and will watch out for them as if they were my own brothers. I know all of them and care for them very much."

Halian studied everyone before looking at Alex with friendly eyes. "We'll allow the seventeen-year-olds to go."

Happiness welled up inside her, but she had to contain her joy. "That's wonderful, Halian. Now that I have your permission, I'll get in touch with the park for final approval. I'll let you know as soon as I have word. Thank you."

She left the pueblo and headed for her parents' ranch, located halfway between Albuquerque and the Zuni land that bordered it. When she reached home, she discovered her mom and dad hadn't returned from town yet. Too restless and excited to stay in the house, she saddled up her horse and rode Daisy to the top of Sunset Butte.

From here she could watch the sun fall behind the mountains. At this time of evening, the sharp play of light and shadow brought out the rich purple and orange colors, outlining the topography that first inspired someone to call New Mexico the Land of Enchantment.

Taking in a breath of sweetly scented sage, Alex dismounted and sank down on a slab of rock to savor this first triumph. The stretch of real estate from this vantage point and beyond included a pueblo, ruins, camps and Zuni petroglyphs and artifacts, some dating back three hundred to fifteen hundred years. This had been her playground growing up. Both she and her mother had Zuni friends and had learned to communicate in their Shiwi language.

On the east side of their vast property sat an old Spanish fort and mission. All of it made up part of the Orange Mesa Ranch. It was just one of the legacies from her mother's great-grandfather, Silas Trent, an entrepreneur who grew up on a ranch in California before buying land here. Thanks to him, Alex was able to use the money from his legacy for a worthy cause.

It was humbling to realize that she'd built up enough trust for the tribe to allow her to try something unprecedented. She hoped the experience would expand the boys' vision of the world, that is *if* the good Katchina gods were listening and decided to be kind.

Though a daring plan, in her heart she was sure Chief Rossiter wouldn't turn her idea down. Besides, as her mother had often reminded her, a Trent didn't fail. Alex couldn't allow her project to fail, not when she'd be responsible for so many precious lives. She'd met with the teenagers and knew every one of them was eager to experience a new adventure.

Jumping up from the rock, she mounted Daisy and headed back to the ranch house, ready to put the second part of her plan into action. After handing her mare over to Chico to take care of, she hurried inside the house, intent on finding her father. First however, she made a detour to her room for the eight-by-ten envelope sitting on her computer table.

"Dad?" She knocked on his study door.

"Come on in, honey." Now that he was no longer a senator, John Harcourt was compiling his memoirs for publication.

Alex slipped inside his office, which looked more like a library with books shelved from floor to ceiling. She coveted his collection on John Muir, the naturalist explorer who wrote about Yosemite.

But since her dad was a history buff, he had other enviable collections of books covering the civilizations of the world. She often found the graying blond father she loved poring over tomes dealing with the American Constitution.

She put her arm around his shoulders and placed the envelope on his desk. "When you fly to California in the morning, will you find out who's in charge of the volunteer program at the park and put this in his or her in-box as soon as you reach Yosemite? Will that be a problem when you're only going there in an advisory capacity this time?"

He pushed his chair back to squint up at her with fatherly concern. "I made a mistake to take you there the first time."

"Please don't say that. I love Yosemite! Whenever I tell the teens what it's like, they get excited to see it, too. You're the one who helped me appreciate how vital Yosemite is to our world."

"I did that?" He sounded surprised.

"You know you did when you introduced me to John

Muir's writings. Once I got started reading, I couldn't stop. I'll never forget something you quoted from him about the giant Sequoias. That hit me hard."

"In what way?"

"I don't have the quote memorized, but the point was that God had cared for all those trees through the centuries, yet only man could destroy them with his sawmills and that was what man left to the American people."

"You remembered that?"

She nodded. "From then on, whenever we went to the park, I used to look at those trees and weep for the earlier devastation. I read more of Muir's writings and developed a love for the place. If tourists could visit Yosemite and see what he was talking about, it might make people around the planet more careful about how they treat our mountains and forests."

Her father reached for her hand and squeezed it. "I should have asked you to write my speeches."

She chuckled. "Think what it would do for the kids to see all the places Muir talked about, especially his journeys into the Hetch Hetchy Valley! I've dreamed of taking some of them there for quite a few years now."

"I have no doubt it would be a wonderful experience for them," her father said. "You've explored it so thoroughly, I think you would live there if you could."

"*If* being the operative word, right?" She tried to play it light. "I've just come from the tribal council meeting. They've finally given permission for me to take a group of boys to the park to be volunteers for the summer."

She could tell her father was surprised and pleased. "You've been working on that a long time. That's quite a coup, honey. A great honor in fact. I'm very proud of you."

"Thanks." She opened the envelope containing her proposal. On top of it was her résumé, which she pulled out. "Take a look at it and tell me what you think. Will Chief Rossiter be impressed?"

He carefully perused the contents like he would a bill that had passed the house. She noticed how thorough he was being.

"Well," he finally said, sounding faraway. "It's as good as any I've seen. You've presented yourself as someone bright and interesting with all the potential in the world. Of course, he knows you well and is already aware of your unique qualities."

"But?" She'd heard the hesitation in his voice.

Her dad sat back in his swivel chair and removed his bifocals. "I know how involved you are with the Hearth and Home project for the tribe, but I also know you've had a serious crush on Cal Hollis for years."

"Cal was a ranger at the park. That's because he saved your life, Dad."

"The pain turned out to be indigestion, not a heart attack."

"At the time we didn't know that. I'm afraid I was like most girls with Cal, guilty of hero worship."

In fact it had been a lot more than that. A year ago March she'd sought him out and had made a fool of herself. When she'd gone back in May, she hadn't been able to find him and was afraid he'd stayed away from her on purpose. The whole experience was humiliating.

"Except you're almost twenty-seven now. It's long past time to let the fantasy go."

"Oh, I've let it go, Dad," she assured him. Cal had made certain of that. It had been over a year since she'd laid eyes on him. There was nothing more pathetic than the ex-senator's pesky daughter literally throwing herself at him. She'd been deluding herself for years that he was interested. If she had the chance to work at the park this summer, she would prove that she was over an infatuation he'd never wanted or encouraged.

"When I bring the kids back to Albuquerque in August, if not before, I plan to work for Hearth and Home full-time."

He studied her for a moment. "You sound like you mean that."

"I do," she said on a sober note. "Law school isn't for me."

"I think I've known that for a long time." One eyebrow lifted. "Lyle Richins will be back from the military by then."

"I know. We stay in touch through email." Lyle was one of the ranch hands and a rodeo champion who'd taught Alex how to ride. He was a great guy.

"Do you think something might happen there?"

"I suppose it's a possibility." She couldn't do any better than Lyle. Alex knew that.

He cocked his head. "Does your mother know the tribe has given its approval?"

"I'm going in the kitchen to tell her."

"She's a huge fan of your idea."

Alex gave him a quiet smile. "She told me it was the first positive thing I've done for myself in years. You know her old rant about failing to plan. I decided to adopt her wisdom and came up with the idea to give the boys this experience—it could be life changing for them. But now it has to become a reality. All I ask is that you get this application in the right basket.

"I would have sent it through the mail, but the tribe has taken so long to make a decision, and now it's too close to the deadline. Will you help me?" She put the résumé back in the envelope with the rest of the papers and sealed it, then wrote *For the Volunteer Program* on the front with a felt-tipped pen.

"Do I have a choice?"

"Dad—" She kissed his cheek. "Thanks for being so wonderful. You don't know what this means to me."

THOUGH THE PERIODIC TRIPS to Cincinnati to be with family were always enjoyable for Ranger Calvin Hollis, he inevitably found himself itching to get back to Yosemite. For the last year they'd been begging him—especially his older brother, Jack—to give up his job and rejoin the family business, Hollis Farm Implements, in Ohio.

They'd assumed his loneliness after losing his ranger wife in an avalanche twelve months earlier would make him receptive to the idea. But they were wrong. Six years ago he'd been transferred in from Rocky Mountain National Park and had loved Yosemite on sight.

It was home to Cal.

With the promise that he'd fly out to see the family in another five weeks, he'd returned to California anxious to feast his eyes on Yosemite's unique grandeur once more. What a joke! Since his arrival yesterday afternoon it had been raining cats and dogs.

He'd read in several journals that the idiom probably came from a British writer centuries earlier. "It was raining frogs and fish" was the more scientific expression because of actual sightings. Just the other day a woman in Australia had found fish in her yard after a heavy downpour.

Whatever, the fact remained that Yosemite was under a mid-May deluge that would probably go on all day. You'd never know Half Dome was out there, looming over the valley. He could only hope the huge tarp he'd used to cover all his earthly possessions he'd packed in the bed of the truck was doing its job.

His Xterra SUV was back at Wawona, his former base. He'd leave it there until he knew where he was being transferred. Chief Rossiter had sent out an email for him to report to headquarters at Yosemite Village by eight sharp Saturday morning with all his gear.

Cal was surprised Vance could get up that early. He was a daddy for the second time, the first being when he and his wife, Rachel, had adopted Nicky, her cute, hilarious nephew.

Rumor had it the head man wasn't getting any sleep. All the rangers laughed because Vance went around with a dopey grin on his face, showing everyone pictures of his little boy, Parker, a dead ringer for him. Cal couldn't imagine being that happy, not when he'd become a widower within two weeks of his marriage.

He checked his watch. Only five more minutes to get there, but in this sodden weather, the road into Yosemite Village had to be driven with caution. Sometimes a black bear looking for cover crossed the highway at the wrong moment. In his view there were too many accidents like that.

As for the rain, it might just have dropped a few

precious frogs on the road, blown off the high alpine lakes by strong winds. They would land startled, but alive. By now most of the smaller inhabitants of the forest had gone under cover, but Cal had turned on the truck's brights anyway.

His reverence for all God's creatures, large or small, caused him to go out of his way to make sure they stayed alive, especially the frogs. Their species had been diminishing for years.

Some experts swore the worrisome loss of the park's amphibian population was due to cyclical fluctuation. Others believed pesticides were the culprit. There was evidence that California's prevailing winds carried farm chemicals sprayed in the San Joaquin Valley eastward directly toward the park, permeating the skins of the frogs and preventing them from breathing.

Those two possibilities could contribute to the decline, but Cal suspected there were others no one had figured out yet. As a park ranger, he'd come to feel that everything in nature was part of a master design. He could *try* to find solutions that made a difference, but that was all.

More from instinct than actual sight, he turned onto the road leading to headquarters. Closer now, he could see there weren't many people around. A few standard-issue government trucks, little else, which meant no tourists to speak of yet. That was a plus.

He pulled into a parking area near the front, shutting off the headlights and the motor. Forget putting on his parka. The thing was sopping wet from all the trips he'd had to make from the cabin to the truck. His hat wouldn't be much help, but he shoved it on anyway and made a dash for the entrance.

"Hi, Cal!"

Ranger Davis covered dispatch and reception. He turned in her direction. Couldn't miss that Southern accent. She had a cute way about her. "Hey, Cindy... how come you don't look like you barely survived the Yosemite monsoon?" He took his hat off to shake the water from it before putting it on again.

"It's called 'rain gear,' Ranger Hollis. Something you've obviously never heard of." But she gave him a warm smile. "The big guns are in the conference room," she informed him. "What's going on?"

"Heck if I know, honey," he teased, mimicking her accent.

"That's bull and you know it!"

"What kind of bull did you say that was, sugar?" Everyone liked Ranger Davis. She had an easy disposition and had been friends with both him and Leeann.

"Oh—" Her face scrunched up. "Get out of here!"

"I'm gettin'!" With a laugh he headed for the conference room.

Closer to the door he spied Vance's middle-aged secretary coming full-speed ahead. "Need some help, Beth?" She was juggling two trays of foam cups full of hot coffee.

"I'm all right, but maybe you wouldn't mind bringing the doughnuts and napkins. They're sitting on my desk."

"Tell the boss I'm helping you, so he won't mark me late." Her laughter followed him as he headed down the hall for her office outside Vance's inner sanctum. He found three cartons and a bag of napkins. Since he was starving to death, he lifted the cover on one box and stole a chocolate doughnut with chocolate frosting.

By the time he entered the conference room, he'd devoured it. Beth took everything from him and set things out on the table against the wall. "There's chocolate on the side of your mouth," she muttered.

"Which side?"

"Try both."

"Am I bad?" He grabbed a napkin to dispose of the evidence. "Now how do I look?"

"If you're fishing for compliments again, you won't catch any here."

He laughed and put his hat down on another side table. From the sound on the roof, you'd have thought it was raining nails. The room had pretty well filled up. Cal took a seat at the large, oval conference table between two of his favorite people, Ranger Mark Sims and Ranger Chase Jarvis, assistant to the chief. Both were talking on their cell phones.

Chase, looking dry and comfortable, glanced at Cal's wet uniform. His eyes gleamed in amusement as he ended the call.

"Don't you start on me," Cal warned.

"I wouldn't dream of it. I pulled all-night duty, so I haven't had my baptism yet. How was your trip home to Ohio?"

"The best in ages. Thanks for giving me the time off."

There was only one problem with going home. Life was flying by and his parents weren't getting any younger. It played on his guilt, but if he moved back, he knew in his gut he'd be unhappy. He'd come through the worst of his pain over losing Leeann. Being out in nature, doing what he loved most—it had been helping him to heal. He didn't want to be anywhere else.

"I'm glad you took it," Chase said, breaking into his thoughts. "Everyone needs a vacation now and then."

"You're right. I plan to take more of them so I can stay in close touch with my family."

"I'd say you're lucky to have them." Chase had been an only child and his parents were no longer alive. "Come talk to me later and we'll work out a schedule for the rest of the year."

"Thanks, Chase."

The district rangers seated across the table grinned at Cal in his wet shirt. He smiled back, then caught sight of Ranger Thompson walking through the door. Jeff had been the first responder to reach Leeann when the avalanche struck near Tioga Pass. Cal had been in another part of the park at the time.

His friend had worked like a madman trying to dig her out. Leeann had had avalanche training, but when they'd recovered her body, she couldn't be revived. Jeff's selfless sacrifice had bonded the two men, who'd already been friends.

They exchanged silent greetings. Judging by the question in Jeff's eyes, he was curious about this meeting, too. Something was up.

Vance entered the room on Jeff's heels, followed by Bill Telford. The superintendent's presence confirmed something important was about to happen. Once everyone was seated, the Chief surveyed the group.

"Good morning, gentlemen. Thanks for coming out in

this beautiful spring weather we're having." Cal chuckled along with the others. "We've said our farewells to two veterans who are already enjoying their retirement. Now it's time to welcome their replacements. After talking it over with Superintendent Telford, I'm pleased to announce the following promotions.

"District Ranger Thompson, who's been stationed at Tuolumne Meadows, will be our new Chief of Resource Stewardship, facility management, roads and trails. Jeff's unique background and skills make him the hands-down choice for the job."

Cal couldn't have been more thrilled for his friend. He clapped harder than anyone. No one deserved it more.

"The second promotion might not come as a surprise to Ranger Hollis, who was told last evening, after returning from a trip, to vacate his cabin in Wawona so another ranger could move in."

Though Cal heard the Chief's words, he couldn't quite believe what they meant.

"For the past seven years Cal's been the assistant to Paul Thomas. Now that Paul has gone, the sacred job of watching over our flora and fauna falls to Calvin Hollis. I can think of no one better qualified than he is to serve as the park's chief biologist. His views on the reasons why our bears are using Hondas and Toyotas for cookie jars will be part of the agenda for our next regularly scheduled meeting."

Everyone laughed and clapped.

Vance smiled at them. "Congratulations, gentlemen. Both of you will be a welcome addition at headquarters. I don't have to tell you what a privilege it has been for me to work with you. I anticipate a long and successful association in the future. You're a great asset to our community here in the Valley."

Incredible that this promotion had come on the heels of his hard-and-fast decision to stay at the park, Cal thought. He loved his family, but being a ranger was his lifeblood.

The Chief's brows lifted. "Speeches can come at the dinner planned in your honor. We'll make that on Saturday the twenty-eighth at the Ahwahnee *after* you've had a chance to absorb the headaches you've inherited."

Both Jeff and Cal groaned in amusement.

"Once we enjoy the treats Beth has provided, Ranger Jarvis will help you make the transition here. Your offices are ready for you to clutter at will. You're both off duty until tomorrow to get your lives in order."

There was no one like Vance. He always cut to the chase, short and sweet. Cal never wanted to work under anyone else.

After a round of hand shaking, everyone helped themselves to the doughnuts. Chase slipped Cal some keys. "The one with number fifteen goes to your house, the other to your office here. I've already given Jeff his. We're all going to be neighbors," A half smile broke out on his face. "I'm warning you now. The wives are already planning to de-bachelorize you, Ranger Thompson."

Jeff grinned. "Not me."

"Tell *them* that." Chase flicked Cal a private, compassionate glance. "For a long time my life looked bleak, too, then a miracle happened. You never know what new events are in store."

Cal watched the ranger walk out of the room.

In Chase's case that was true. He'd been a man with

amnesia. When he recovered years later, he was united with Annie, the woman he'd loved. They had a daughter, Roberta. Life was glorious for him.

Cal's situation was entirely different. He was glad he was being moved to new housing. For the last year he and another ranger had been sharing the little cabin where he'd lived with Leeann for two short weeks. Memories lingered. He needed to make new ones. This change would help.

Because of his promotion, he could now implement some of the programs he'd been planning. Speaking of work, he looked around. The conference room had emptied except for him and Jeff. Since the announcements had been made, it was back to business as usual.

"Is your truck outside?"

Jeff shook his head. "I came in early to get the key and drive over to the house. We actually have garages now. My stuff's still waiting to be unloaded."

"So's mine, but my truck's right outside. I'll drive you home and help you, then we'll go to my place."

"I have to run by my new office first. I left my rain gear in there."

Cal plucked his hat from the table and followed him down one hall and around the corner to the second door on the right. When Jeff unlocked it, he made a disapproving sound in his throat before putting on his parka and hat. "Talk about empty—"

"Don't worry. You heard the Chief. You'll have your signature on this place in no time." Cal's office was at the other end of the hall. After reporting to Paul on a regular basis from Wawona, he didn't need to see it. Tomorrow would be soon enough.

Chapter Two

The parking lot was crowded when Alex pulled into the post office. Her parents' mail was delivered to the ranch, but she had her own post office box.

It had been close to a week since her father had returned from Yosemite. He said he'd put her envelope in the basket for the person running the volunteer program. The only thing left to do was wait for a reply. Already it felt like months.

When she unlocked the box and found the usual bunch of travel brochures and junk mail, her heart plummeted. Discouraged, she walked over to the nearest waste receptacle to discard them and almost missed the envelope she'd been looking for. It had been sandwiched in among the pamphlets.

National Park Service.

Alex tossed everything else before opening the letter with trembling hands. Please, please be good news.

Dear Ms. Harcourt,
Thank you for your interest in becoming a volunteer for the summer at Yosemite National Park. Our office has reviewed your application. Before

any decision can be made, all interested parties must meet in person with the head of the volunteer program. This screening is in place to ensure this is a good fit for you and a good fit for the park.

The following date of Monday, May 23, has been reserved for interviews. First come, first served, 8:30 a.m. to 5:30 p.m. Report to the Department of Stewardship and Management Facility at Headquarters in Yosemite Village.

That was two days away! She'd barely gotten in under the wire. If she hadn't sent the application with her dad, it would have been too late.

Alex ran out of the building clutching the letter in her hand. She had a ton of things to do before she flew to Merced tomorrow. First on her agenda was a stop at the beauty salon in the mall.

"All this hair?" Darlene looked aghast. "You're joking! I thought you told Michael you'd never get it cut. If I recall, the last time he took off a quarter inch, you had a meltdown."

I've changed since then.

"That was the old me, Darlene." Hopefully she'd changed in a lot of other ways, too. "The new one wants to look twenty-six, not like a nineteen-year-old teeny-bopper. Turn me into today's confident woman," she teased. "Chic but feminine, with a touch of class, yet not overstated. Maybe a trifle windblown?"

Darlene grinned. "You don't want much, do you?" She rummaged around and found a chart with the latest short hairstyles. "Take a look at these while I get my hacking shears."

Alex knew the one she wanted the second she saw it. "This." As soon as Darlene came back to the chair, Alex pointed to the midlength bob. The ends were slightly curved, with longer side-swept bangs.

"With your oval face, that would look good on you. Your hair's thick enough. You can wear either a zigzag or straight part."

"Let's do it."

After years of being called Rapunzel by her friends, Alex was ready to have Darlene lop off her long mane. The stylist went to work. When she'd finished and was applying a touch of hair spray, Michael returned.

Alex saw him in the mirror. He held up her long locks to his ears like braids. "I think I'll use these for Mardi Gras. What do you think?" He batted his eyes.

Both Alex and Darlene laughed.

He held the skeins of hair in his hand. "Many women want to achieve this silver-gold color. If I could find a way to bottle yours…"

Removing the drape, Alex got out of the chair to look at him. "What do you think? Honestly."

Michael cocked his head while his eyes examined her. "*I* think I don't know who you are anymore. Who are you trying to hide from?"

He saw a lot, but he had it wrong. It was Cal who had hidden from her. That had devastated her, but she'd had a year to get beyond the pain. "It's more a case of hoping people will see the grown-up me from now on, someone to be taken seriously."

His smile grew thoughtful. "Interesting. Try a little more bronze in your lipstick. Tone down your eye makeup. Your eyes are green enough already. Don't use blush unless you're going out in the evening. You don't need it. With hair and glowing skin like yours, natural is better."

"I agree," Darlene said.

Whoa. But Alex had asked for honesty. Whoa. "Thanks, both of you. I mean that sincerely." She put a hundred dollars on Darlene's table next to the brush. "Now wish me luck."

She left the salon feeling pounds lighter, both mentally and physically. While she walked through the mall to the sporting goods store, she kept seeing herself in the glass, unable to believe it was really her.

"Hi," she said to the female clerk. "I'd like your help in choosing an outfit for an interview at a national park. I'm hoping to get a volunteer job. I need something sensible, yet sophisticated."

"There's a cotton sweater that's just been put out in a dark olive green. It has a collar and short sleeves. Come over here. We've paired it with pleated pants in a tan twill. It's a lovely look and would suit you. But if you don't like green, the sweater also comes in burgundy, burnt orange and Persian blue."

Alex didn't hesitate. "The green's perfect. I'll try it on."

"What size shoe do you wear?"

"Seven B."

When she came back out of the dressing room, the clerk showed her a pair of women's Avia low hiker boots in dark brown suede and leather. Alex put them on. They felt and looked good. After picking out socks, a couple of pair of jeans and a similar number of short-sleeved tailored blouses in tan and cream, she said, "I'll take everything. You've been a real help."

One more stop at the department store for a new lipstick and she drove back to the ranch, already feeling transformed. Her brothers would tell her it was long past time her old hairdo and high-maintenance designer wardrobe were gone.

That evening she put on her new clothes—a style she'd never worn before—and walked through the ranch house to the kitchen. Her parents were seated at the island enjoying coffee and some of the cook's grasshopper pie. So much for the diets they claimed to be following.

One look at her and they both cried, "Honey—" almost falling off their stools. The double take they gave her said it all.

"I'm glad you're speechless. That means I've accomplished my first objective. Here's the reason." She handed them the letter. "I want Chief Rossiter to believe in me and my proposal."

They read it together before her father looked at her through new eyes. "You get my vote, honey."

"What are your plans?" her mom asked.

"I'm flying to Merced in the morning," Alex said. "I've booked a room at the Holiday Inn. Monday morning I'll rent a car and drive to Yosemite Village for the interview. I don't want to be seen hanging around before."

Her blond mother with her perennial tan slid off the stool to hug her. Muriel was well built and stood five foot seven. Everyone told Alex she looked like her mom. "Good for you, honey. You're there for business, no other reason. Now you're learning. May the best woman win."

ONE MORE CARTON TO GO.

While Jeff was bringing in more things from the truck, Cal opened the box and started shelving the last of the books in one of the bookcases he'd put in the study. These were textbooks he'd used while attending the University of Cincinnati, first for his undergrad in biology, then his MBA. It all seemed another lifetime ago.

On the other wall he'd placed three floor-to-ceiling rattan wine racks. They were perfect to hold the many maps he referred to on a day-to-day basis. Each one covered different quadrants of the park.

His last task was to reassemble his long drafting table and floor lamp. He needed a big surface to spread out his work. Once he'd accomplished that, all he had to do was set up the computer and his study was complete.

This was the first time he'd lived in a house since leaving the farm at eighteen to go to college. For years he'd rented apartments while he'd been in school and after he'd joined the family business. Later he'd gone to work for the forest service and ultimately the parks, where he'd lived in a succession of tents and cabins.

This three-bedroom home was luxury by way of comparison. How ironic that he had so much more space now and no one to share it with him.

"I've never seen this oil painting before. Where do you want me to hang it?" Jeff stood in the doorway.

Cal knew the painting he meant and didn't bother to look up. "Just set it against the wall in the spare bedroom with the other boxes I need to go through." The picture of the San Miguel Chapel in Santa Fe had been a special thank-you gift from Senator Harcourt after his visit to the E.R. at the San Gabriel hospital in Stockton, California, three years ago.

His daughter, Alex, had been with her father, who appeared to have suffered a heart attack while on a hike in Dana Meadows at the eastern end of the park. Cal had been the one to do CPR and get the senator flown to the hospital. Alex had been so frightened before the doctor told her he'd only suffered severe indigestion that she'd broken down in Cal's arms, unable to thank him enough.

She'd filled his arms in a way that surprised Cal, but she'd been too young for him. The Chief reminded him she was the senator's daughter in a not-so-subtle hint to keep his hands off her. Unfortunately there had come a time a year ago when he'd crossed a line with her and vowed to himself it wouldn't happen again.

By that time Leeann Grey had been transferred to Yosemite. She and Cal had known and liked each other when he'd worked at Rocky Park, but he'd only been there a few months before he'd been sent to Yosemite to work under Ranger Thomas. They hadn't had the time to explore what might have been between them.

When Cal saw her again a few years later, he was already settled into his work, enjoying his career. They began dating and one thing led to another. Leeann was an attractive brunette his own age who'd shared his love of the outdoors. The timing was right and they got married.

He hadn't seen Alex Harcourt since his wedding, but the mention of the painting brought an image of her instantly to mind. Something told him she'd picked out that gift. Her father had been born and raised in Santa Fe, which meant the subject had great meaning for their family. But Cal had never hung it. Now that he had a real home, he'd get around to doing some decorating and find a place for it.

Jeff appeared in the doorway again, jarring him back to the present. "Where do you want the box marked personal?"

"Same place as the other boxes—in the spare bedroom." Those contained family pictures and photos of the rangers, including wedding pictures of Leeann. "One of these days I'll find the time to sort everything out. Maybe next week."

Gathering the empty boxes, Cal walked down the hall. Jeff was just coming out of the other bedroom with a load. "No more work," he told him after they'd put the cartons in the back of the truck. "Now that we're both moved into our houses, let's get out of here. I'm starving."

"You're not the only one!"

The rain had let up, allowing them to walk to Yosemite Lodge for dinner in the dining court without getting drenched. Afterward they went back to Jeff's house around the corner from Cal's to kick back with a few beers and watch a movie.

Cal only made it halfway through the film before he knew he needed a bed in a hurry. When he looked over at Jeff, the guy was passed out on the couch. Cal got up and turned off the TV. After a minute's debate, he decided not to wake him and took off for his house. If it seemed strange to go to sleep in different surroundings, he didn't notice. Physical exhaustion had caught up to him.

AT NINE ON MONDAY MORNING, Alex pulled into the parking lot of the Yosemite Lodge under an overcast sky. There were a lot of cars. Some of them had to belong to applicants like herself.

Though the summer tourist season wouldn't officially start for a few more days, the park attracted vacationers year-round. Alex ought to know. She'd come here so often, she could give guided tours. In fact she'd played up that aspect in her proposal, but didn't mention that she'd learned the equivalent of a university course of valuable knowledge from Cal.

His insights had given her a reverence for the park, particularly the animals. Every time she listened to one of his talks, her appreciation for its wonders grew.

Well…this was it.

She reached for her handbag and got out to cross through the village area to headquarters. When she walked inside, a few tourists were milling about, looking over the displays and maps. Alex approached the female ranger in reception. She'd seen Ranger Davis on duty many times before.

"Hello."

The other woman's head came up with a smile. "Hi! Welcome to Yosemite."

"Thank you. I'm supposed to report to the Department

of Resource Stewardship for an interview. My letter didn't give me a specific time, only the date."

"Oh, yes. You're one of the applicants for a volunteer position. What's your name?"

"Alex Harcourt."

The ranger's brows knit together. "I didn't know Senator Harcourt had an—another daughter."

Alex heard her near slip of the tongue. The woman was going to say an 'older' daughter. Alex's change in appearance was better than wearing a disguise. She couldn't have been happier about it.

"I'm afraid I'm his one and only."

Ranger Davis looked puzzled. "I didn't recognize you without your long hair." That wasn't all she didn't recognize, Alex was sure. Her change of wardrobe had to be a shocker—from trendy tourist to the practical garb of national forest service worker. "Just a minute while I ring Ranger Thompson and let him know you're here. I believe he's in with someone else right now. Take a seat."

"Thank you." Alex walked over to one of the chairs to wait. Instead of looking around eagerly in the hope she'd see Cal, like she used to do, she reached for one of the brochures about the park attractions. The last thing she wanted was to make eye contact with any of the rangers who'd stonewalled her a year ago when she'd tried to find him.

The minutes wore on; forty-five had passed before she was told to walk down the corridor and make a right turn at the next hallway. Ranger Thompson's office was the first door on the right.

Alex thanked Ranger Davis and made her way through

a group of visitors to her destination. The door had been left open. No one was inside the room. It looked like a receptionist's office, small, with a few family pictures and a mug with pencils on the desk. No sooner had she sat down than another door opened from an adjoining room.

An attractive ranger with dark brown hair stepped inside. Alex had seen him before. "Ms. Harcourt?" He walked around the desk to shake her hand. "Over the past few years we've run into each other coming and going, but never officially met. I'm Ranger Thompson. I hope you didn't have to wait too long."

"No, no. It's fine."

"Good."

If he was shocked by her changed appearance, he was an expert at hiding his feelings, or else Ranger Davis had alerted him so he wouldn't react. Either way, his inscrutable expression gave Alex nothing to go on but her grit.

"My assistant, Diane, screened all the volunteer applications and sent out the letters. Give me a minute to find yours and look at it." He took his place behind the desk and searched through a pile of newly tabbed folders until he found hers.

After studying the contents he said, "Your résumé indicates you've taken college classes in both the U.S. and Europe. You speak fluent Spanish and have had some amazing travel experiences—a safari in Kenya, a trip to the hidden rain forest of Madagascar. I also notice you've won some awards barrel racing that are very impressive."

"Thank you."

"It seems that between classes and travel, you've worked part-time for Hearth and Home in Albuquerque, New Mexico, for at least ten years. Was that for your father?"

Her father's seven terms as a U.S. senator would have opened many doors and given her ample opportunity for work. Naturally this ranger would assume as much, but she could tell he wasn't bowled over by anything he'd read yet.

"No. With my mother. If you'll look beneath the application you'll see the proposal I've worked up." His assistant, Diane, had seen it. Otherwise Alex wouldn't be sitting here.

He shot her a puzzled glance.

"I'm sure you've never heard of the Hearth and Home program. There are twenty H & H ranches built all over our family's property outside Albuquerque. Here's a brochure that will explain everything." She took it from her purse and handed it to him.

As he started to read, she watched his expression change. A minute later he looked up at her sharply. "Your mother did all this?"

"It was her brainchild funded by the Trent foundation, the legacy from her great-grandfather. I've worked alongside her all my life and helped run it. These families are my friends."

Alex could hear the pride in her voice. "Several years ago I saw an article put out by the Lost Trails of the Sierra Youth Fund asking for volunteers for Yosemite and a light went on in my head. What I'd like to do is bring some teenagers from our Hearth and Home families to help here."

He sat back in the chair, his steepled hands pressed against his lips. She noticed he wore no rings. "Go on."

Perfect. She'd captured his attention.

"My father has shared the park superintendent's and the chief ranger's concerns that minorities aren't attracted to the national parks in big numbers to work or visit. It occurred to me that by bringing in these English-speaking Native Americans, it'll serve the same important purposes of the LTSY volunteer program. As I understand it, they have three aims—to develop future stewards of the park, to help do vital restoration and to give the kids a completely different kind of employment than any they've known."

His hazel irises flared as if she'd suddenly dropped in from another planet.

"There's nothing like exposure to nature to fire up young minds and give them vision. They know how much I love Yosemite and have expressed an interest in being part of such a project. The Trent Foundation would provide the funding, of course. Ten thousand dollars per teen for the summer. This money has been earmarked for me personally to use throughout my lifetime. It has nothing to do with my father or mother.

"And I'd like you to know that Dad had nothing to do with my idea or this proposal. He's retired. If you decide it isn't right for the park, please don't be concerned that he'll pressure you to change your mind. And contrary to what you're probably thinking, the superintendent doesn't have a clue, either. What goes on during this interview is between you and me only."

Alex didn't want to belabor her point, but it was

important to establish up front that this was her own initiative.

"Because Dad is the former head of the Federal Energy and Natural Resources Committee for the Senate, I'm aware that other national parks have the same problems and needs—and offer the same programs—but I thought I'd start with Yosemite because I love it here."

Taking a leaf out of her mother's book, she got to her feet to make a dignified exit after a short, concise presentation. "If you think you're interested, you have my phone number and email address on the application. Thank you for your time, Ranger Thompson."

"Please sit down, Ms. Harcourt," he said unexpectedly. "Chief Rossiter needs to hear this before any decision can be made. It's possible he's available now."

Alex couldn't be happier. Adrenaline surging, she waited while the ranger made a phone call. After a brief conversation he hung up and said, "Unfortunately he's not in the building. Could you be back in my office at nine in the morning? He'll be available then."

"Of course. Thank you."

THE HILLS ON THE OUTSKIRTS of Redding, California, housed the Cascade Bear Institute of California run by Gretchen Jeris. She was a bear biologist who'd figured out there had to be a way to co-exist with bears without killing them. After years of research, she'd found a solution in the Karelian Bear Dog and brought it back from Finland.

On Monday morning, Cal drove to Redding to pick up the bear dog he'd been matched with after a complicated screening process. Today he'd be taking him home.

Cal had been up here several times before to undergo training under Gretchen's exacting standards. All bear dogs were different from each other. All handlers were different. It was critical that the dog's personality matched Cal's in order to ensure the highest potential for compatibility.

Gretchen had dedicated her life to breeding the best dogs and promoting their use through other agencies around the world by sharing her training protocol. The litter Cal's dog came from was sired by her prized Finnish dog, Paavo Ahtisaari, an international champion from a line of champions.

The primitive breed was known for being exceptionally intelligent, brave and kind, but even in a litter, not all were considered to be bear-conflicting dogs. Gretchen watched for that special pup, born with the quality of fearlessness and aggressiveness that made it able to track and handle bear and moose confrontations.

With their quick reflexes and instincts, Karelians could put a bear to flight with no problem and attack with great pugnacity if necessary. They would sacrifice their own lives for their master or whatever they guarded. In that regard they needed special training to learn to hold back for the safety of others.

The dogs were used in many areas of the U.S. and the world on a small, experimental basis, even for a time in Yosemite. For several years Cal had talked to Paul Thomas, his former boss, about the possibility of introducing them into the park again and making them a permanent fixture. Besides dealing with bears, they were excellent for catching bear and deer poachers, a problem the rangers had to deal with on a continual basis.

Paul would have been willing to let Cal go ahead, but the old superintendent wasn't keen on the idea, so it was tabled until he retired. Once Telford was appointed superintendent he was much more willing to listen. Yet it was still hard to find funding.

The park was always looking for private donors and couldn't function without them. After Cal came across two butchered bears last summer in the Hetch Hetchy Valley, he'd told Paul he'd donate his own money to get a KBD project started. Paul cleared it with Telford and Cal was finally given the go-ahead.

Now that Cal was in charge, he had hopes that once the public saw the dogs' value in the park, private donors would step up with funding. Karelians would not only help him track the persons guilty of killing bears, but protect the campgrounds and still allow the bears to live out their lives in their own habitat.

Since Gretchen had known Cal was coming, she was waiting for him when he drove in and walked him over to a roomy pen housing three dogs. He hunkered down next to the four-month-old pups. Mostly black with some white markings, they stood with their pointy ears erect, reminding him of young huskies.

On the family farm in Ohio, Cal had always had a dog, but his work since then had prevented him from owning one. He felt as excited as a little kid at the prospect of caring for this new puppy.

Gretchen explained that these three had come from the same litter. She opened the cage and brought out Sergei, who knew him immediately from his prior visits. Cal chuckled because the pup's action aroused the jealousy of the other two.

"Sergei? You and Ranger Hollis are about to bond as partners in life." She put him on a lead. "Go ahead and walk him for as long as you want before you have to go."

He studied his new dog. Sergei seemed to stare at him, as if he were transmitting his thoughts to Cal's mind in that uncanny way some animals had. "You want to go home with me? You want to follow me around and hunt bears?"

This dog would eat, sleep and go to work with him. Cal spent most of his time out of doors, and training Sergei would be an ongoing process, one skill at a time as he learned to socialize with hundreds of people on a daily basis.

Cal tested Sergei with a few commands and the dog's responses were remarkable. He walked Sergei back to the cage. Gretchen had gone inside to play with the other dogs but she saw him coming.

"I should have introduced Sergei's brothers, Yuri and Peter."

When he laughed she admitted, "I like the Russian composers."

"So do I."

"The breed prefers its own kind and these three love being together, but they're not bear-conflict dogs like Sergei. He's unique. They're going to miss him. So will I."

She closed the pen and they finished up their business. Just like a new baby, a puppy required a lot of paraphernalia. Cal had brought a tarp to throw over everything in case it started to rain.

Sergei went into his new crate in the back of the truck

without a problem and Cal loaded the truck bed with the rest of the supplies. Gretchen gave him enough food and supplements for two months. "This is Eagle Pack holistic select dog food, a high-end brand with nutrients rich in protein."

Along with toys and a whistle, Gretchen gave him a dental and vet kit that included drugs and sutures. She told Cal he'd find them useful if he was up in the mountains and an emergency occurred. Cal was trained and licensed to handle drugs, which made sense when there was no vet around.

"Call me if you have any questions." Gretchen handed him the envelope with Sergei's papers, including his vet exams and shots.

"I'm afraid you'll be hearing from me a lot."

"That's good. I'd rather you check in with me than go your own way on something and have to retrain later."

"Understood. It's been a privilege, Gretchen." After thanking her for everything, he slid behind the wheel of the cab and took off for the park with his precious cargo.

Halfway home Alex Harcourt came into his mind again. She was the person he had to thank for urging him to get the bear dog he wanted. When he'd talked about the dogs being used in other parts of the world, she'd argued that if he'd always wanted one and believed it would benefit the park, then surely his boss wouldn't say no. Because of her continued interest, he'd approached Paul about it the first time.

One thought about Alex led to another. He wondered what had happened to her in the past year. By now she was probably married to some hotshot attorney from an

Ivy League school, the kind of man her father wanted for her.

When Cal had been chosen to show the senator around the park on various visits, he'd heard all about the older man's plans, especially when the senator brought his daughter with him. He'd used that time to instill his hopes and dreams in Alex, and Cal had been a reluctant observer.

Cal realized he was driving too fast. Chastising himself, he slowed down to the speed limit. For a ranger to be caught in uniform speeding down the freeway with a rare, primitive breed of dog in the back would be great PR for Yosemite, the kind that gave the Chief nightmares. Anything to do with the park, good or bad, was picked up by the media.

Before long Cal pulled into the driveway of his fifties ranch house, part of the community of modest housing for the rangers set among the pines. As he'd learned since moving in, his dwelling had come furnished with the bare necessities—a bed, a couch, coffee table, a couple of easy chairs, a kitchen table with two wooden chairs and a washer and dryer. But it was up to Cal to turn the house into a home, which he hadn't had time to do yet.

He got out of the cab and immediately undid the tailgate to attend to the dog, who couldn't wait to be released. Like Cal, he preferred open spaces.

While Cal attached the leash, he heard children's voices. Next door was Ranger Farrell, whose wife, Kristy, was a schoolteacher who worked for the Mariposa Country school district and taught the kids living in the park.

Without intending to, Cal had arrived just as the

children were getting out of class for the day. It was a good thing because the dog's socialization with children was especially vital.

There were a dozen in all, including the Farrells' cute little seven-year-old, Brittney. They took one look at Sergei and came running over. Thirteen-year-old Brody King was in the lead, followed by Nicky Rossiter and Roberta, Chase's daughter.

"Hi, guys," Cal called. "Come and meet my new dog. His name is Sergei."

"Cool," Brody declared. The oldest of the kids, Brody walked right up to the dog to scratch its head. The younger ones gathered round, anxious to get a turn.

"Sir what-did-you-say?" Nicky had a way of cracking everyone up, including Cal.

"Ser*gei*. It's a Russian name."

"He's so cute." Roberta made maternal sounds. "What kind of a dog is he?"

"A Karelian Bear Dog." Cal couldn't wait to hear what Nicky had to say to that.

Brody's head came up. "Did you get him from Russia?"

"No. He was born here, sired by a champion bred in Finland."

Nicky frowned. "How come you didn't get an American dog?"

Cal choked back his laughter. "Because this one is trained to frighten bears away."

At that revelation the children cheered and decided they wanted one, too.

"I'm glad you live by me!" Brittney piped up.

"He's not as big as a mama bear," Nicky observed.

"Sergei doesn't have to be. His job is to shepherd a bear away."

"How?"

"Well, once he's learned to track a bear's scent, I'll put him to work when a bear is reported in a campground area. I'll take him there on leash and Sergei will sniff around and indicate if the bear is still there, even if none of us can see it. Sergei's not a hound, but he's fearless. The whole point is for him to harass the bear and make enough noise that it won't want to come anywhere near a campground again. You don't need a big dog to do that."

Nicky looked at Roberta. "My mutt's scared of everything. I've got to go home and tell dad. When he finds out, he'll buy *us* one." He took off like a shot.

Cal decided this was a good time to break things up. Sergei needed to run. "See you guys later."

Cal headed for the forest a couple of blocks away. Sergei stayed right with him. They played hard before returning to the house. Cal kept him on leash while he carried everything inside, and once he'd emptied the truck, he closed the door and let Sergei loose to investigate his new surroundings.

By dinnertime, the dog knew every inch of the house and where to find his food and water in the kitchen. Until Sergei was a little older, Cal would crate him at night.

Before he fixed a meal for himself, he gave the dog a beastie toy to play with. Inside the fleece pouch was a piece of real bear fur, and Sergei got all excited by the scent. They played tug-of-war in the L-shaped living room until Cal got hungry.

He rested the toy on the drop-leaf table propped

against the wall in the kitchen, but that was a mistake. Sergei jumped right up on top to get it. Cal ordered him down and walked him to his crate in the tiny third bedroom. Obedience lesson number one.

After downing three sandwiches and a quart of milk, Cal went into his office to look at the usual bunch of reports emailed by the other rangers. After a while, he decided Sergei had been in the crate long enough and went to the other room to let him out.

The dog lay beside him, his head resting on his front paws, while Cal took care of the remainder of the day's business. When he'd finished his work, he praised Sergei and gave him a doggie treat from his pocket. "You know what? It's just you and me from now on. I'm going to train you to sniff out deer poachers, too. You'll be a multitasking miracle." Sergei wagged his tail at Cal's words. "Come on. Let's take another walk."

Chapter Three

"Mom? I'm glad you were able to answer right away."

"I've been waiting for your call, honey. So...did my daughter knock the ball out of the park yesterday? No pun intended."

Alex chuckled. "Ranger Davis, the receptionist, didn't recognize me. That alone got me to first base. Once I was sent back to Ranger Thompson's office, he pretended not to notice that my whole appearance had changed. He was very polite and treated me with the utmost courtesy before he questioned the nature of my work experience. At that point I directed him to the proposal he hadn't read yet."

"And?"

"He told me to be at his office at nine this morning to talk to someone else. As I shut the door, he was still sitting there looking stupefied."

"Marvelous! Where are you now?"

"Almost at headquarters. If things don't turn out, I've decided to go to work full-time for Hearth and Home."

"I know. Your father told me."

"Now that Dad's retired, he'd like to have you around more."

"You mean after he's worked all day on his book? Honey…you don't have to worry about your dad and me. We're figuring things out as we go."

"So am I. The work at Hearth and Home is what I know and do best."

"Dare I say that if your proposal is turned down, I'm delighted at the prospect of my daughter spending more time on a project that, except for my own family, has been closest to my heart?"

"I know. I love the Zuni families, too. If by any chance this proposal *is* turned down, I'm going to send applications to some of the other parks like the Tetons or Yellowstone. Now that the tribal council has given their permission, I'd be horrified if I had to tell them my idea was rejected."

"It doesn't sound like you failed to me, otherwise you wouldn't have been asked to show up this morning."

Alex bit her lip. "You're right. I love you for supporting me in this, Mom. Whatever happens, I'll be in touch later today," she added before hanging up.

Ten minutes later she entered headquarters, but this time she didn't need to ask Ranger Davis for help and walked straight back to Ranger Thompson's office, where she discovered his assistant.

"Hi!" The woman greeted her with a smile. "You must be Alex Harcourt. I'm Diane Lewis."

Alex liked the charming African-American right off. "Nice to meet you." The two women shook hands.

"Ranger Thompson has arranged for you to meet with Chief Rossiter. I have to tell you I was impressed with your proposal. If you want my opinion, it was brilliant."

Alex couldn't have been more pleased. "Thank you."

"If you'll go back out and take the other hallway, it's the second door on your left."

She knew where it was. "I'll find it." As she made her way to his office, Alex had to tamp down her excitement.

The minute Vance's secretary, Beth, saw her, she said, "I like your new hairdo, Alex."

"Thanks. If I'd known how light it would make me feel, I would have had it cut a lot sooner."

Beth laughed. "The Chief has someone in with him, but he'll be free in a minute. Would you like coffee?"

"No, thanks. I had some on my way here."

"Forgive me for staring, but the change in you is lovely…and dramatic."

"When Ranger Davis saw me yesterday, she thought I was the elder Harcourt daughter."

"So did I for a second, but I didn't know until just now that you had a sister."

"I don't. But I do have two blond brothers who look more like my dad than I do." She'd had another brother, too, but he'd died.

"In other words you take after your mom. She must be a beauty."

"Thanks for the compliment. She's definitely that. My dad was smitten the first time he saw her ride in a rodeo."

"Do you ride, too?"

Alex didn't have time to answer because the inner door opened and a powerfully built, uniformed ranger entered her line of vision. He had a dog with him. Alex stood up to make room for them to pass, but it was the wrong thing to do and startled the animal.

"Sorry," she said and backed herself against the chair. When she looked up, her world suddenly spun away. Cal—

"Ms. Harcourt," he said quietly.

It had been a year ago March since she'd last seen him. Now it was the end of May. The sight of those familiar blue eyes and dark blond hair caught her lungs in a vise so tight she couldn't breathe. The last time she'd looked into them they'd blazed with heat.

This morning she saw no fire in them. Instead they had a guarded quality. He looked stunned to see her and was studying her as if she were some kind of Yosemite petroglyph he'd unexpectedly come across and was determined to identify.

With one encompassing sweep, he took in her appearance. She was wearing the same outfit she'd put on yesterday for the interview. She knew that nothing about her was the way he remembered, and it seemed to frustrate him.

He frowned as if his eyes were playing tricks on him, and Alex felt a rush of satisfaction that her transformation had rocked him.

Looking down, she noticed the black dog with white feet and chest rubbing up against Cal's leg. Alex loved dogs, especially Charlie, their family's border collie, who'd died of old age recently.

"Well, look at you..." She leaned over to pet the dog. "With those pointy ears, you're a darling." He licked her lips, making her laugh. "Ooh, that was a *nice* kiss." At first she couldn't identify the breed, then memory and recognition kicked in. Alex lifted her head. "You finally got yourself a Karelian Bear Dog! That's what he is, right?"

Cal nodded with seeming reluctance. "You have an excellent memory." He'd spoken in a quiet voice just now, but she remembered other times when it had been deep and vibrant while he gave lectures to the tourists. She would never forget its husky tone when he'd cried her name in protest before kissing her.

"Only because you used to talk about owning one someday."

"Sorry he got frisky just now. I'm still training him."

"That's all right." She rubbed his head again. "He kind of looks like a husky. What's his name? I feel like I should call him Nanook or something."

"It's Sergei."

His dog stared up at her with adoring eyes. "The Russian name suits him. Considering the semimonastic life you lead, Sergei ought to be a wonderful companion. He seems devoted already. I'm happy for the two of you and sorry for all those bears he's going to harass. Now if you'll excuse me, Chief Rossiter is waiting for me. Have a great day, Ranger Hollis."

Always before she'd called him Cal, without his permission of course. But not today, not in front of Beth. Judging by his frozen, rugged countenance, probably never again. He really wasn't happy to see her. What more proof did she need to stay out of his way?

Intent on her destination, Alex walked inside the chief ranger's office. The breath didn't leave her lungs until she'd closed the door behind her. Alex was proud of herself. She'd behaved like a woman in charge of her world and happy about it. In fact she'd played it just right.

For the first time she'd walked away from *him!*

She'd showed confidence, not arrogance.

She'd been indifferent with a smile.

Having learned a brutal lesson at his hands a year ago, she'd been ten steps ahead of him today.

Chief Rossiter stood up. He always had a ready smile. The head of the park was as gorgeous as Cal, in his own way. "It's nice to see you again, Alex. Your new haircut suits you."

His sincerity meant a lot. "Thank you."

"You and I have a great deal to discuss. Come and sit down."

"Does this mean you think my proposal has merit?" She shook hands with him before taking a seat opposite his desk.

"It has more than that. I liked it so much, I told Jeff to hire you."

Her eyes smarted at his faith in her, but she fought to keep her composure. "You have no idea how much this means to me. The boys don't know what they're in for yet, but after they've been here for a few days, they'll probably never want to leave."

"Men after my own heart."

She smiled. "Just so you know—the tribal council didn't feel the girls should participate yet and they're only allowing sixteen boys to come. I know the park policy is to encourage equal opportunity. Give me a little more time with them."

He nodded. "After my dealings with Chief Sam Dick

over the years, I understand completely." Alex had met the venerable Piute chief and his wife several times. They were marvelous people. "I understand this was your idea from start to finish."

Ranger Thompson hadn't left anything out. That was good. "Yes."

"Thank you for coming to Yosemite instead of Yellowstone first," he teased.

To Alex, there was no one like Chief Rossiter, a brilliant man in her opinion. Serious when he had to be, he possessed a terrific sense of humor, too. Everyone loved and respected him.

"It's my favorite place."

"And mine," he echoed. "How would you like to do another job for me while you're here overseeing your young volunteers?"

She blinked. "What do you mean?"

"When Rachel first came to the park with Nicky— before she was my wife—I offered her the job of being my liaison. She turned me down flat."

Alex laughed. "That's because she wanted another job more. She told me that in private."

His eyes danced. "Beth used to be my liaison, but I needed a good secretary, too, so the liaison position never got refilled. It requires a certain personality I haven't been able to find. When I was reading over your inspirational idea, it came to me that you'd be perfect for the job."

Curiosity was killing her. "What does it entail?"

His expression grew more serious. "To be my eyes and ears while you're out and about in the park in your volunteer minibus. It will provide the perfect cover for you. When the teens are at work, you'll be free to mingle and observe what goes on around here—good and bad. Document what you see with a time and date and report back to me personally."

Whoa. "You want me to spy?"

"In a word, yes."

When she laughed, he did, too, but she knew beneath that laughter he was serious. Somehow she'd earned his trust. How incredible.

"I need someone who looks at things outside the box so to speak, someone who's very savvy about internal problems here at the park, but isn't a ranger or a worker at one of the concessions. Because of your father and the many visits you've made with him, you have inside knowledge that can't be gained from a textbook or a lecture. You're also fearless and know the park well."

"Will anyone know about my...side job?"

"Besides Beth? No. It will be our secret, otherwise there'll be no point to it." Alex couldn't argue with his logic. "I'd only be able to pay you an entry-level wage, but if you accepted, you'd make me a happy man. But please don't think that if you turned it down, I'd change my mind about your proposal."

The Chief wouldn't have asked her to do this if he didn't think she could be valuable. She liked the idea that no one else would know about it, even Cal. Chief Rossiter had given her a new feeling of confidence, as if she really belonged here. Alex felt indebted to him. "I know you wouldn't do that. If you think I can be of any help, I'll be happy to do it."

He flashed her a smile. "Excellent. When you need

to talk to me, Beth will fit you in. She'll also give you a paycheck every two weeks."

That would be a novelty she welcomed. "May I ask your advice about something?"

"Of course."

"What would you think if I went by the name Alex Trent? Whatever happens this summer, good or bad, I want to function on my own recognizance, not my father's."

His eyes shone with approval. "That's very commendable, but I don't see any reason for you to do that. Your father's been retired close to two years, and he's out of the limelight now. While you're working here, you'll be part of the woodwork, so to speak."

She grinned. "That's true. You've relieved my mind."

"Good. Now tell me how you came up with the wonderful idea to bring those boys to the park."

NO SOONER HAD CAL GONE off duty and returned home than he heard a familiar rap on the door. He'd left a voice mail for Jeff to get back to him, but a personal visit was much better. Seeing Alex today had blown him away. With her father no longer coming to the park, he'd assumed he'd never see her again.

She'd caught him off guard for a number of reasons. Besides the amazing change in her appearance, he hadn't seen a ring on her finger. It had been over a year since he'd last seen her, and he wouldn't have been surprised if there was a change in her marital status by now.

He removed Sergei's leash, but at his command the dog stayed next to him as he walked into the hall to open the door. Jeff stepped inside with an envelope under his arm. "Sorry I couldn't get back to you until now. I've been in a ton of meetings. The last one just broke up."

His eyes swerved to Cal's new buddy. "Hey, Sergei— I've heard about you for a long time. We meet at last." After putting the envelope on the front hall floor, he hunkered down to get acquainted with the dog and rub his white chest vigorously. "You're not so big. Hard to believe you're already old enough to scare off a bear."

"We're working on it," Cal said, shutting the door behind him. "I was about to make dinner. Do you want some?"

"I grabbed a bite about an hour ago. Thanks anyway."

"Then come all the way in and sit down."

Jeff picked up the envelope from the floor and followed Cal into the living room. Sergei sniffed around him. "He's cute. If you poured white paint all over him he'd—"

"Look like a husky?" Cal finished for him. *Alex had said the same thing.* "My thoughts exactly."

Jeff continued to examine the dog, leading Cal to believe he was buying time for a reason. Cal thought he knew why. "When I came out of Vance's office this morning, Sergei and I literally bumped into Alex. At first I wasn't sure it was her."

Cal was still in shock from the change in her looks and her attitude. He'd sensed something different about her, as if an invisible shield had gone up. And the way she'd looked right through him had thrown him.

"I know what you mean," Jeff agreed. "She'd been in

my office first. Now that she's all grown-up, she's turned into a real stunner."

She always was. Yet over the past year Alex had morphed into an ultrafeminine woman with a figure that did amazing things for the conservative clothes she'd been wearing. Without all that glorious hair, her classic features were more prominent. Her eyes reflected the green of hidden summer vales high in the mountains.

"Alex told me she had an appointment with the Chief," Cal said. "I didn't see her father around. What gives?" He and Jeff had no secrets where Alex was concerned. His friend finally stood up.

"What gives is the answer to one of those prayers Chief Sam Dick told Vance the gods must have heard."

The hairs went up on the back of Cal's neck because the old Piute from the Hetch Hetchy Valley was still a powerful force throughout the park. Vance had been a boy when Chief Sam had shown him where he used to hunt acorns. Those two shared a bond as binding as blood.

"That important, huh?"

"Yup. I have to tell you I've never been more surprised." He handed Cal the envelope. "Everything you want to know is in there. I'm going to leave it with you because I've got some business to do at the house, stat."

"I'll walk you out." Sergei followed them.

Before Jeff left he said, "Give me a call later when you've read through everything."

Adrenaline surged through Cal's veins, but not from excitement. The Alex he'd known had changed on some level he didn't understand, and he was uneasy about what he'd find in the envelope.

"Don't forget tomorrow!" Jeff called from his truck. "The new adult summer volunteer staff will be going through orientation. You're scheduled to address them in the conference room at eleven."

"Diane alerted me," he answered, but his thoughts were far removed from park business. Once he closed the door, he rubbed the dog's head and went into the kitchen for a cup of coffee.

"Okay, Sergei. Let's see what's in here." He pulled the contents out of the envelope.

Application for Yosemite Park Volunteer Program was the first thing to meet his eyes. The moment Cal saw the name *Alexis Trent Harcourt* printed on the line, the blood pounded in his ears, cutting off all sound except his own heartbeat. *Unbelievable.* This meant she was going to be here all summer.

He studied the info on her application form. At first nothing came as a surprise. He knew about her travels and her stab at some college courses. But a barrel racer? She could ride? That was something he hadn't known.

Cal reached for the brochure beneath. He read it through and let out a long whistle, his brow furrowing in disbelief. Some of the traveling Alex did was to visit orphanages around the nation with her mother?

He read through her proposal, taking it all in. His brain did the math on the funding. He wheeled around, startling Sergei, who scrambled to his feet, ready for anything. His mind racing, Cal grabbed his cell phone to call Jeff, who picked up on the second ring.

"I thought I'd be hearing from you pretty quick.

Quite a surprise when you thought you'd seen the end of her."

Surprise wasn't the right word. Everything in her proposal came as a revelation. "In all the years Alex has been coming here, she never said a word about this part of her life, and not a peep from the senator."

"That shouldn't come as news to you, Cal, not when you tried to avoid her as much as possible."

"You know why. She was too young to take seriously, but today she turned the tables."

"What do you mean?"

Cal told him what happened outside Vance's office. 'I felt like I'd been drawn through a matrix, not knowing up from down. After Alex gave Sergei a good rub, she disappeared inside the Chief's office as if I didn't exist."

"Well, at least you no longer have to worry she's back at the park because of you."

Nope. While Cal digested the ramifications of that remark, Jeff added, "I have to tell you I don't believe I've ever seen Vance this excited about a new project."

"Naturally. Her inspiring proposal is an answer to any prayer whether it be from the Zuni, Paiute or rangers' god."

"Who'd have guessed what was going on beneath that mane of hers?"

Like gold shot with silver in the moonlight...

Cal inhaled sharply. "This is a coup for you, Jeff. You're the chief steward of park resources. When Telford hears about this, he'll go back to D.C. and put Yosemite on the map as the model of the future. You'll be famous for hiring her."

"Just what I always wanted," he said with a rare display of sarcasm. "That's why I became a ranger. Her ability to fund everything is a surprise, though. I thought the senator was the one with the family money."

"So did I."

"I did a little research and learned they live on the Orange Mesa Ranch outside Albuquerque. Silas Trent bought up 800,000 acres and turned it into the sixth-largest cow-calf operation in the States."

That explained her riding abilities. "And all along I thought I knew what made her tick," Cal muttered. "Where are you going to house her and her group?"

"At Sugar Pines campground with the volunteers from the LTSY fund. Everything's in place. Alex has been preparing her teens for the last couple months. There's no problem accommodating her group. Some of the other groups will stay at Tioga Pass. We wish there were more volunteers coming."

Cal shook his head in amazement. Sugar Pines was in the Yosemite Valley, where many of the eight hundred miles of trails throughout the park needed restoration. The volunteers lived in the cross-country ski facility during June and July.

Speaking of skiing, Cal said, "Did I ever tell you about the incident one winter when she and her friends went off the ski trail and got lost? She phoned the ranger station and asked me to come and rescue them. She used to show up at the damnedest times and places."

"That was probably before I was transferred in. Did you comfort her?" he teased.

"*I* was the one who needed comforting, Jeff. Her unexpected appearance at the park without her father around scared the hell out of me, and you know why. In front of the Chief, Senator Harcourt made it clear he trusted me with his daughter, if you know what I mean."

"Afraid I do."

"I'm surprised her self-centered nature hasn't gotten her into more trouble by now," Cal grumbled.

"How did she know which ranger station to contact?"

Cal let out a caustic laugh. "You tell me and we'll both know. Maybe some Zuni magic rubbed off on her when she was little."

The thought gave him an odd shiver, but the situation was different now. How strange to think of her overseeing a bunch of teens while he was out chasing bears all over the park with Sergei.

"Well, you've got a new partner to warn you when she's around. He's more powerful than magic. Be thankful for small favors."

Cal rubbed his jaw. Things had changed. He knew in his gut he didn't have to worry about Alex anymore. "See you tomorrow, Jeff. Thanks for bringing her proposal by. I'll make sure it gets back on Diane's desk in the morning."

After they hung up, he fixed a sandwich, then took Sergei outside one more time. When they returned he crated the pup and got ready for bed. But when it came time for sleep, Cal tossed and turned.

For the first time in a year Alex filled his thoughts rather than memories of Leeann. Over the seven years Cal had worked for the park, the senator made regular visits. Whether winter, spring, summer or fall, he was often accompanied by his daughter, a fashion plate with hair down to her waist.

In the beginning, the twenty-year-old was a royal pain who thought she could get away with murder because of her high-profile name and looks. She knew she represented the gates of paradise to every young, red-blooded male in sight.

It was this immature, spoiled rotten, pampered, blond vamp of a daughter who early on became Cal's nemesis. At least that's what he'd told himself in order to stay away from her. But that had pretty well been impossible because her visits increased in frequency, making him more and more aware of her.

On the March afternoon she'd found him alone at the lookout tower near Glacier Point, she'd thrown herself at him one too many times and he'd decided to give her what was coming to her and send her running. To his shock the reverse had happened and he'd lost control.

The incident shouldn't have happened.

Meeting up with Leeann again had been providential. He began spending exclusive time with her, and before he knew it, they were married. But now Leeann was gone and Alex was back, this time for the whole summer.

So what's it to you, Hollis? The way she blew you off today, you have nothing to worry about.

Chapter Four

Diane stepped up to the lectern. "After a ten-minute break, we'll resume your orientation."

Alex checked her watch. It was quarter to eleven. A dozen summer volunteers, both male and female, had been hired by the park for various jobs. After everyone was introduced and they'd watched a PowerPoint presentation about the park given by Ranger Thompson, half of them got up from the conference table. She decided to stay put.

Cal could be anywhere in the park, but in case he happened to be around headquarters, she didn't want to bump into him again by accident and have him think she'd planned it on purpose.

Unfortunately one of the new volunteers in the group seated at her right had already glommed on to her. Brock had spiky black hair and was probably in his late twenties. Not bad looking, and he knew it. When she made no move to leave the room, he remained seated, too.

"So, Alex Harcourt...where have you been assigned with your youth group?"

"Sugar Pines campground." Ranger Thompson had already designated the ski facility for her boys. It was near the village, which would be a good thing because she could keep a close eye on them after hours.

"I'm going to be helping at the Crane Flat campground" came his unsolicited response. Thank goodness that camp was near the western perimeter of the park, away from hers. "But when I'm off duty there's a ton of stuff to do around here."

"That's true." She'd done most of it.

He smiled into her eyes, his interest clear. "Where are you from?"

"New Mexico."

"Don't you want to know where I come from?"

Alex was counting the minutes until the meeting started up again, but she didn't want to be rude. "I was just about to ask."

He gave her a crooked smile that probably worked on most females. "Las Vegas."

"What brings you here?"

"I do freelance photography."

"Then you've come to heaven on earth."

"You can say that again," he murmured as he studied her features.

Oh, please...

To her relief people started coming back in the room. Jose Martinez, a fit-looking Latino probably in his late thirties, sat down on her other side. During the introductions, Diane had indicated he would be helping at Half Dome, where a majority of tourists congregated daily to make the steep ascent using the cables.

Alex purposely struck up a conversation with him in Spanish, knowing it would irk Brock, but she didn't want him getting any ideas about her. He needed to find someone who was looking for a good time. There were enough attractive women around.

Out of the corner of her eye she saw Diane walk into the room. "It looks like everyone is back. We'll now hear from the chief biologist of the park, Ranger Hollis."

What?

When had Ranger Thomas retired?

That meant Cal worked here at headquarters instead of Wawona.

Alex's hungry eyes fastened on Cal as he entered the conference room, keeping his dog on leash. With his tall, hard-muscled frame, no one filled out a uniform the way he did. His eyes were the kind of intense blue that almost made you tear up when you looked into them.

At thirty-four, he was a gorgeous man with an unmistakable aura of authority. It didn't surprise her that he commanded the interest of everyone in the room, male or female.

She knew the second his gaze fell on her, but she'd already gotten out her loose-leaf notebook and stared at the paper, poised to take notes while he lectured.

"Good morning," he said in his deep, compelling voice. "Let me introduce you to Sergei, my Karelian Bear Dog. When you see us around, you'll know he's learning how to track bears and help keep our campgrounds safe.

"You've been given materials about the flora and fauna of the park," Cal continued, "but the bears deserve some discussion for a few minutes. Tourists come to the park to see our American black bears. Keep in mind that few of them are black. They come in a range of colors from brown to cinnamon to blond. There are close to five hundred of them. They'll be mating through June and July, making them more aggressive, and will eat anything day or night. Unfortunately, once they've tasted human food, they want more. Here at Yosemite we're dedicated to eliminating the temptation. As volunteers, you'll be expected to educate anyone you see not using the designated canisters and food storage lockers."

Alex had heard all this from his lips before. He was so good at what he did and had a great way of communicating his passion for the park and its inhabitants to others.

"The bears are expert at rummaging through trash cans and campsites and breaking into cars to get at any food, even the tiniest crumbs around a child's car seat. They get spoiled and love to sit in one place and eat and not have to work to find food. The problem is, bears and people don't mix well, but the traditional methods of dealing with problem bears, like shooting them with rubber bullets or other nonlethal rounds, only meet with limited success.

"Even when the bears are trapped or tranquilized and removed to the wilderness, more than half get into trouble again. Some have to be killed, and killing goes against everything I, and all of us here at the park, believe in. The black bears and Yosemite are synonymous as far as we're concerned.

"To banish or kill them isn't the answer. A solution needs to be found that will encourage a peaceful coexistence and preserve both humans and animals. These dogs are part of that solution, since experiments have proved they have an eighty percent success rate at keeping bears away from campsites. But your help as volunteers is needed to educate the public how they can contribute, too."

Cal was a natural teacher and had his audience mesmerized. That was exactly the way he'd affected her the first time she'd laid eyes on him.

The dark blond, six-foot-three bachelor, happily married to his work, probably didn't make more than $36,000 dollars a year. No house of his own, he moved from ranger tent to lookout tower to cabin, depending on his latest assignment. On call, day and night.

For six years she'd had a crush on him that was so bad, she'd feared it had turned into a permanent condition. From the beginning there'd been an instant attraction. Lust at first sight. Electrified by a pair of blue eyes.

She'd been introduced to him by the former superintendent of the park, who'd been friends with her father. At twenty she'd felt quite grown-up and resented it when the hunky ranger had treated her like a teenager.

He'd been twenty-seven at the time—not *that* much older than her. That's what she'd told herself back then—when she had little knowledge of life except to know when a guy found her attractive. Ranger Hollis had been no exception. That electrification had happened to him, too.

Though he'd been careful, she'd caught him checking her out after she'd joined the group of tourists he was addressing about fishing regulations. A man could hide a lot of things, but he had the kind of eyes that ignited with inner heat when emotions caught him off guard. Like the time she burst into his tent unannounced to let him know she'd arrived back at the park. He'd gotten rid of her fast, but not before she'd seen that flare of interest.

Over the years she'd lost count of the number of times she'd watched his gaze charge up when he happened to see her coming. Or when he approached her. She remembered the time she and two of her close girlfriends had come here to ski. By accident Carol had led them away from the trail in the designated ski area and they became lost. Alex called the closest ranger station for help.

It had thrilled her when Cal showed up with another ranger. She hadn't planned for them to meet while she was out with her friends. The warmth in his eyes when he'd first seen her was real, even if he'd quickly repressed it.

That was the trouble. While she talked and flirted with him, he went along to a point, but treated her like she was someone's little sister. All the time he was pretending to be amused, she knew deep down he found her attractive, yet he never let anything get out of hand. He never touched her. She could get so far with him, but no further.

There was only one time when he'd revealed another side to her. It was the last time she'd seen him. After learning from another ranger that he was at the lookout tower, she'd surprised him. "I brought you something from Paris," she'd called to him, climbing the steps.

It was early afternoon. They were alone.

In a stern voice he told her he was on duty at his post until further notice. "No tourists allowed."

She kept climbing until she reached the top and moved toward him. He warned her the risk of an avalanche was too high in that area for her to be there. "You shouldn't have come."

When he ordered her back down, she lowered the picnic basket to the floor. Feeling reckless she said, "Make me." At that point he took hold of her arms and dragged her toward the stairs. But she refused to cooperate and went limp against him.

"Damn it, Alex," he muttered just as she lifted her head. It was the first time he'd called her by her first name instead of Ms. Harcourt. Desperate for this closeness, she pressed her lips to the hard mouth she'd been craving for years, blinded by her own desire for him. Suddenly the man who'd always controlled their relationship was out of control.

He crushed her right up against his chest, kissing her with an intensity that fueled her response. If he'd been trying to teach her a lesson, it had failed. As seconds ticked by, their kiss burned hotter and deeper, ramping up the emotions driving them. She had no doubts that if another ranger hadn't chosen that moment to climb the stairs, forcing her to vacate the premises, they'd have spent the night together.

The result of their unexpected encounter had been disastrous. The next time she went back to the park to see him, he wasn't available. No one would tell her where she could find him, and that hurt because he'd kissed her as if his life depended on it. Probably at his request, the other rangers had closed ranks on the ex-senator's daughter, making her feel like a pariah.

It was bad enough that Cal had felt that way about her, but if his peers were purposely shunning her, too...

Wounded by the experience, she hadn't gone near the park for a year, and had fallen into a depression even her parents had noticed. She'd done nothing but prove she was a shameless flirt who'd outlived her welcome at the park.

She'd needed to erase the image, but it meant going back to the scene of the crime. To her everlasting gratitude, Chief Rossiter had given her the opportunity to prove her worth. Now was her chance to show everyone she'd grown up.

While she was immersed in torturous thoughts, everyone at the table started clapping. Cal's speech was over. She busied herself putting away her paper.

"We'll break for lunch, then reconvene at one o'clock," Diane said from the podium. Cal had already left the conference room.

It irked Alex to feel Brock staring at her. To put him off, she shifted away from him in the chair and pulled out her cell to make a phone call, hoping he'd get the point.

"Where are you going to eat?"

Alex couldn't believe his persistence. It crossed boundaries and turned her off completely. "I'm not," she said over her shoulder before the harried-sounding person on the other end of the phone answered.

"Buses For Sale—"

"Hello. I'd like to speak to Randy in the detailing department, please."

"Just a minute—"

Before she could say thank-you, he'd put her on hold. The customer-service guy must be having a bad day.

When Brock made no move to leave, she got up from the chair and walked over to the large picture window that looked out on dense forest in the distance.

"This is Randy."

"Hello, Randy. It's Alex Harcourt. How's the H & H logo coming on the minibus?"

"It'll be done Friday."

"That's wonderful. I'll be flying into the Merced airport on Saturday morning from Albuquerque and will pick it up then." The boys would be with her. Only three more days…

Something black-and-white flickered in her peripheral vision. It was Sergei in the entry to the room, and behind him was his owner.

WITH THE DOOR AJAR, CAL could see into the conference room. He'd been waiting for Alex to come out in the hall, but she was on the phone. Since the Chief wanted her on board and it was now a fait accompli, Cal realized they needed to talk. The sooner the better, considering she'd avoided looking at him throughout his presentation.

Their strange past history had to be buried. He wanted the air cleared. For that to happen, they needed to be alone, but the male volunteer who'd been sitting next to her showed no signs of leaving. If he'd made a lunch date with Alex, that was too bad. Cal didn't have much time before he started on his afternoon rounds.

He reentered the conference room with Sergei at his side. As he drew closer, he could have sworn his presence intimidated her. She wasn't behaving like the Alex he'd known. That was his fault, but things were about to change.

She spoke into the phone for a few more seconds, then clicked off. "Ranger Hollis…I didn't realize you were waiting to see me."

"Ms. Harcourt? If you don't mind stepping into my

office at the end of the hall? It will only take a few minutes."

She nodded and walked around the table to get her purse and handouts.

"Excuse us," he said to the other volunteer, who sat there clearly miffed.

"Sure."

Cal wasn't impressed with the other man's attitude. Something didn't seem right about him, but at the moment he had Alex on his mind. When he left the room to walk back to his office with Sergei, he could sense her behind him. As soon as she entered, he shut the door and invited her to sit down opposite his desk.

When he took his place in the swivel chair, the dog lay down beside him. "I'm sorry if I interfered with your lunch date."

"No problem. There'll be other opportunities." So the guy *had* made plans with her. "Ranger business has to come first. By the way, congratulations on your promotion. It's well deserved."

"Thank you." He could feel his frustration level rising. This wasn't the way he'd envisioned their conversation going. "Alex, we need to talk. It's been a long time in coming."

"You're right. I'd like to start with that incident in the lookout tower. What happened was my fault." She spoke the words with unexpected frankness. "I'm deeply ashamed of my actions. It was totally immature. My brothers figured I'd never grow up, but I'd like to think I'm finally there."

Cal had been right. A new Alex had arrived at the park, one he didn't recognize.

She folded her arms. "Let's agree that every time I came to the park in the past, I made your life miserable. I give you my word you'll never have to worry about me again. Do I have your forgiveness for virtually attacking you in the tower?"

She stared at him without flinching, her eyes as green as the leaves of the flowering dogwoods near the edge of the forest.

He took a fortifying breath. "You know very well there's nothing to forgive. It was just a kiss, one we both enjoyed. I kissed you back, remember?"

"Only because I provoked you. I was a fool. You deserve a medal for putting up with me as long as you did." To his surprise she got to her feet, causing Sergei to lift his head. "Since Chief Rossiter has given me a chance to do something that means the world to me, I promise to stay out of your way." She'd already said that.

"I'm afraid that would be impossible," he informed her, "and that's the reason I wanted to talk to you. We'll be seeing each other all the time. The Chief is excited about your project. We all are. I want your success as much as anyone else around here."

She gave a small smile. "Thank you. Even if it almost gagged you to say it, I appreciate your willingness to forget the past. The truth is, I was a big nuisance, but those days are definitely over. I've got my work cut out with the boys."

He studied her for a moment. "You never told me about Hearth and Home. I'm very impressed."

"It was Mom's creation," she informed him. "I grew up being a part of it because I'm her daughter. Every time I visited the different ranches on our property to help the kids with their English, I'd show them my latest videos from Yosemite. They always wanted to see more.

"I felt guilty that I'd been able to have these priceless experiences and they hadn't, so I decided something should be done about it. But convincing the tribal council took a lot of talking. Several years in fact. Now that it's going to happen, I'm worried it might bomb on me."

"Not if the Chief has anything to say about it." Her green eyes looked so vulnerable that a part of Cal wanted to help, too. Her idea *was* brilliant.

"Thank you, and thanks for the opportunity to talk. I've needed to get this off my conscience since last May."

She was confused. "Don't you mean March?"

She shook her silvery-gold head. Even in the dim light of his office, her hair shimmered. "No. I came to the park in May, but I couldn't find you and none of the rangers could tell me where you were. It was humiliating to realize that I was persona non grata, not only with you but your colleagues. The lesson was one I'd needed for years."

Cal couldn't allow her to go on assuming something that wasn't true. He stood up. "Before you leave, let me make something clear. If the rangers didn't tell you anything, it was because my wife had just been killed in a late-spring avalanche here at the park."

"*Wife—*"

She didn't move, but he could have sworn her eyes dimmed.

"Yes. Leeann was a ranger who'd been a recent transfer from Rocky National Park. We met several years earlier when I worked there, too. The last time you came here, I was in Colorado with her family for the burial. Because of the possibility of negative publicity in the media, especially when it could reflect poorly on the park's safety issues, the rangers were sworn to secrecy."

If he wasn't mistaken, she'd lost some color.

"Your private fraternity is good at keeping secrets. Not even my father heard about it through the head of the federal park committee who took his place. How devastating for you."

"It was."

She frowned. "When I showed up at the tower in March, why didn't you tell me you were engaged? If I'd known, I'd like to think I would have had the decency to leave you alone."

Considering the way he'd kissed her back, she had every right to ask that question. "I didn't propose to Leeann until April. We married in May. She was killed two weeks after that."

During the silence he knew she was counting the days between the tower incident and his marriage. After the way he'd practically devoured Alex that afternoon, it wasn't very long for him to have become involved with someone else, let alone get married.

"I'm sorry for your loss." She sounded so sincere it twisted his gut. Her gaze fell on the dog. "Sergei must be wonderful comfort for you."

At the sound of his name, the dog got up and took a few steps toward her. She stopped long enough to reach down and rub his chest. "Let's hope you turn out to be Yosemite's wonder dog. Your master's counting on you." She patted his head and stood up. "See you around, Ranger Hollis."

Unless he had a reason to request another conference with her—and he couldn't envision that happening—he knew in the core of his being she'd never willingly cross his threshold again. The knowledge should have come as a relief.

After she'd gone, he put his cell phone in his pocket and left headquarters through the back door. Sergei climbed in the truck cab with him, and he started the motor and took off for Big Oak Flat entrance. Time to do the annual inventory of food lockers and bear canister rentals throughout the park.

BY THE TIME THE ORIENTATION ended at four, Alex was confident no one had noticed the agony she'd lived through. There'd been a presentation by Ranger Sims and short talks by various forest service personnel.

She hadn't heard any of it. The knowledge that Cal had gotten married so soon after she'd left the park in March filled her thoughts to the exclusion of anything else. All this time she'd believed he'd purposely avoided her in May.

How narcissistic was that when in reality she had been the farthest thing from his mind! To think he'd been over a thousand miles from the park attending his wife's funeral…

Alex had never met the transfer ranger named Leeann. She supposed that his having known her before coming to Yosemite was the reason they'd gotten married so fast. She must have been an exceptional woman. In his grief over losing her, his new dog, Sergei, would provide some solace and distraction.

Another pain shot through Alex. What universe had she been living in all this time? It was beyond embarrassing. Anyone with brains knew that an infatuation was almost always unreciprocated. In most instances the person was oblivious.

Alex had committed the cardinal sin by forcing her attention on Cal, who'd finally given in like any ordinary male. And he'd immediately forgotten their experience in the arms of the ranger he'd married.

She closed her eyes for a moment, marveling that she'd had the nerve to seek him out and initiate the kiss that had ended up going on and on. Scarlet heat shot through her at the memory of his warm mouth on hers.

If there was one moment in her life to make her thankful she'd been born a woman, that had been it. In that one kiss she'd felt a combination of chemistry and magic she would never know with anyone else. It was agonizing to realize that such a transcendent moment for her hadn't affected him the same way. In a weak moment, Cal might have found Alex tempting, but Leeann had been the one who'd set him on fire.

How strange that a kiss could have such a profound effect on a human being. There had to be much more to it than lips and mouths tasting each other. Billions of people had kissed since the beginning of time. But what ingredient was needed to set off a combustion that both participants felt at the same time.

"Are you staying in the park tonight?"

Brock's question jolted her back to her surroundings.

She shook her head. "No. I'm flying home, but I'm sure we'll see each other again."

"You can count on it."

She got up from the chair, grateful he didn't try to detain her further. She planned to fly back to Albuquerque and get everything ready for Saturday, when she'd be accompanying the boys to the park.

Alex had already made arrangements that when they arrived in Yosemite valley, they would stay overnight at the famous Ahwahnee Hotel where presidents and queens had slept and dined. On Sunday, she would drive the boys to the campground and help them get settled in before they started work on Monday.

After speaking with Chief Rossiter yesterday morning, she'd contacted Halian and Lonan with the good news. Lonan said he would talk to each family to get the boys prepared.

In the meantime she had a ton of things to do, including taking them shopping for clothes and toiletries safe to use in the park. They needed everything from coats and boots to sweats for sleeping. Their suitcases had already been ordered with the H & H logo.

She'd also put in an order for twelve dozen white T-shirts with the words H & H Yosemite Youth Volunteer in a dark green color. Those shirts and jeans would be their uniform. When they weren't at work, they could wear what they wanted.

Before she reached Merced, she called the cell phone store in Albuquerque to make sure her order for three dozen phones with cameras was ready and that service had started. Tomorrow morning she'd deliver them to each family. The boys would be able to download pictures to their families' computers as well as the one at the tribal office so everyone could enjoy them.

The whole trick for Alex was to stay busier than she'd ever been in her life.

Unfortunately her mind wouldn't let go of a certain conversation she'd had with her father last May before she'd left for the park. They'd taken a horseback ride, and while they were out enjoying nature, he'd cautioned her not to go to Yosemite again.

"Why? Mom gave you a hard time for five years before she agreed to marry you. Is this so different?"

He pulled on the reins and turned in the saddle to study her with worried blue eyes. "I don't know. You tell me."

"I've always felt Cal's interest, but suspected there was a reason why he held back. At first I thought it was because he figured I was too young. There's a seven-year difference in our ages. But after a while I began to wonder if he was the type who didn't want to get involved with me because I'm your daughter and you worked too closely with his bosses. I've come up with several other reasons, too."

She looked out over the rocky formations ahead of them. "He only earns enough money to take care of himself. It's possible he's one of those men who would feel emasculated if his wife had more money than he could make in a lifetime."

"Honey, you're not mentioning the one thing that appears the most obvious to me. He could be involved with another woman. You have no idea what he does in his spare time. Maybe he's had a relationship that has gone on for years."

She shook her head. "No. He's always let me hang around him, flirt with him. If he'd truly been in love with someone else, he wouldn't have given me the time of day."

"Some men like to look no matter what."

"I'm aware of that, but Ranger Hollis isn't a player."

"You don't know that."

Headstrong as usual, Alex had gone to Yosemite to prove her father wrong. Today she'd found out John Harcourt had known exactly what he was talking about. Cal had been romantically involved with Leeann over a period of years. Alex's punishment would be to see Cal around the park this summer and not be affected.

Could a person learn to shut off emotion? Probably not, but it didn't matter.

What she needed to do was lose herself in this project she'd created from the ground up.

Naturally she wanted it to be successful. Chief Rossiter was counting on her, but there was much more to it than that. For her it was vital that these wonderful boys who'd come from a totally different culture and circumstances than her own would have experiences in a place she'd always considered paradise. If the time they spent in the park shaped even one boy's future for the good, it would be worth it.

Because of the boys' reverence for nature, Alex was convinced they'd return to their families at the end of the summer enlightened even further. She couldn't ask for more than that despite her personal heartache over Cal. Time was supposed to bring forgetfulness. She'd pray for that.

Chapter Five

Cal had five minutes to shower and change into a clean uniform before dinner at the Ahwahnee. Since Alex had disappeared from his office on Wednesday, he'd put in the hours of ten men while she was back in New Mexico getting her group ready to fly up to the park.

The shocker came last night when he'd awakened out of a dream with feelings of guilt because it was Alex's ardent mouth he could taste and feel, not Leeann's.

Seeing Alex again had brought deeply buried memories to the surface. That surprised him. He'd thought his marriage to Leeann, no matter how short-lived, had made him forget Alex, but that wasn't the case.

He supposed it was natural, considering the fact that he had known Alex much longer than Leeann. There'd been other women he'd had brief relationships with over the years, but none had made a lasting impression—until Alex.

Years ago a girl-woman had painted herself into the canvas of his life. Her hair and eyes added splashes of color more vivid than a silvery-gold Yellowstone Falls cascading through an autumn rainbow, more green than the moist, lush grass growing in the high meadows during late spring.

The guys had teased him about being the object of hero worship. At first he'd laughed it off, not taking it seriously. But the girl-woman had grown up while he hadn't been watching….

By now she and the teens ought to have arrived at the park and were probably getting settled in at the ski lodge.

"Come on, Sergei. We've got to hurry or I'll be late for the dinner the Chief has planned in our honor."

Before long he and the dog entered the dining room with its imposing granite pillars and a thirty-five-foot-high beamed ceiling of sugar pine trestles. Light from the chandeliers reflected in the floor-to-ceiling windows, and linen cloths and china on the tables created an elegant atmosphere in an otherwise rustic setting.

With one glance he noted the place was full of tourists. Seeing this crowd, you'd never know the economy was going through a recession. While he looked around for his colleagues, his eyes were drawn to a woman whose hair seemed to possess a metallic sheen. He'd only seen hair like it on one other person.

She was seated at a table near one of the windows, yet even accounting for the distance separating them, she stood out from everyone else. When she turned to talk to a young man on her left, he caught a glimpse of her profile and the breath was suddenly trapped in his lungs. *Alex.* What was she doing here?

As he stared, he realized she was surrounded by the lean, dark-haired teenagers she'd brought here for the summer. He counted sixteen. They all wore collared shirts and filled two round tables.

Someone waved to him from a nearby table. It took a second before he realized it was Jeff. The guys, including the superintendent, were already gathered with their wives and children.

Cal decided it was no accident Alex was here, or that her party had been placed near the head ranger's. Bill Telford had probably seen to it because he wanted this experiment to succeed. What better way for the powers that be to get acquainted with the teens and make them feel welcome.

He started for his table, but Sergei had other ideas and strained against the leash, almost tugging free before reaching Alex. His dog had licked her once and knew her flowery scent. *So did Cal.*

"Hey—there's Sergei!"

Nicky's voice sounded behind him. Cal looked around. Vance and his wife had just come into the dining room. Roberta and Brody scrambled out of their chairs to pet the dog, creating minor mayhem, and all the other children in the room were staring their way. He turned back to Alex.

By now she'd seen him, but she was looking through him the way she'd done outside the Chief's office, her eyes and features devoid of emotion. A strange shudder went through his body.

"Guys?" Alex said to the teenage boys who were taking it all in without saying a word. "This is Ranger Hollis. He's the chief biologist for the park." She said something else in their native language and they nodded. Then she reverted back to English. "And this is his new dog, Sergei. He's a Karelian Bear Dog who's being trained to frighten the bears away from the campgrounds. You'll be seeing him around all summer. He's very friendly."

All the time she was speaking, Sergei kept rubbing his head against her skirt. She looked stunning in a dusky blue tailored suit, and Cal had trouble focusing anywhere else.

Somehow in his bemused state he remembered to greet the teens. "Welcome to the park, gentlemen." He started around the table, shaking each volunteer's hand. Alex followed and introduced them by name. Sergei lifted a paw for them to shake, too. That made the boys laugh, and they relaxed and talked among themselves.

When Cal came to the last person, he realized the guy was probably around thirty. "This is Lonan Kinard," Alex explained. "He's on the tribal council and volunteered to come and be in charge of the boys."

"Lonan, it's an honor for us," Cal said sincerely.

"For us, too. It's good to meet you."

"We're glad these teens are here for the summer. If you ever need anything, call on me or ask any ranger for help. We always appreciate extra hands at the park and admire you for being willing to come. I hope it'll be a satisfying experience for you." Cal looked out over the group. "Maybe some of you feel the way I did when I first saw Yosemite, like I'd arrived in God's front yard. It's an awesome place to work and live."

The teens nodded with a smile.

Alex lowered her eyes, but he'd glimpsed her suspiciously bright gaze before she sat down. Taking a deep breath, he gave his dog a stern command so he wouldn't linger next to Alex, though he could hardly blame Sergei.

They walked around the banquet table and Cal took a seat next to Jeff. Sergei sank down on the floor beside his chair. "Surprise," Jeff muttered.

"That's putting it mildly," Cal whispered back before starting in on his salad.

"What you did went a long way to breaking the ice with those teens. I'd say your dog is working magic big-time."

Cal agreed Sergei had been picking up tricks fast, but where Alex was concerned, his buddy had a lot to learn about control. Gretchen had told Cal that he and Sergei were a good psychological match. Maybe *too* good. His dog had already bonded with Alex.

"A couple of flashes went off while you and Sergei were making the rounds."

"I noticed." Cal frowned. "No doubt someone on Tel-ford's staff."

"He insisted on being with me when Alex arrived at the hotel earlier with the boys. Once he heard she'd booked rooms for them here tonight, he took over."

That figured.

"From his standpoint this is a dream photo op to ad-vertise Yosemite, but the boys might not be comfortable with the attention yet. If you want to know what I think, from the way he acted around Alex this afternoon, he has a personal interest in her."

Cal wouldn't put it past him. Telford had children in college, but the widower could still be infatuated by a gorgeous woman years younger than him. Alex had come to the park often enough for him to be more than aware of her.

Unable to help himself, Cal cast a covert glance at her. Right now she reminded him of Wendy from *Peter Pan,* telling stories to the lost boys. She had a genuine connection with them.

While she'd been introducing each one to Cal, she'd made little personal remarks that told of their long friendship. Some of his assumptions about her that he now knew had no basis in the truth came back to haunt him. To think she'd been a teacher to these boys over the years, performing a service without any thought of reward.

Alex had done him a favor, too. She'd been right about Cal's decision to get a dog. His subconscious need for a companion had driven him to act and he'd gone to Redding to investigate the possibility. Once he'd seen the new litter of pups, he'd approached his boss, Paul Thomas, for his permission, all thanks to her.

Jeff nudged him in the ribs. "It's speech time."

Cal had been so immersed in thought, he'd eaten his entrée without being aware of it. "I gave mine while I walked around the table talking to the teens."

Once dessert was served, the Chief said, "While we welcome the Hearth and Home volunteers to the park, we're also here to honor two rangers whose promotions are well deserved and equally well underpaid, as we all know."

Laughter broke out.

"If either of you would care to comment…"

"Ranger Hollis already said it best," Jeff spoke up.

"Yosemite is one of the earth's greatest treasures. I consider myself lucky to be a part of it."

"That makes three of us," Vance said in a husky voice.

While Cal was drinking the last of his punch, Alex and the boys had gotten to their feet. All of a sudden Telford stood up. "Don't leave yet, Ms. Harcourt," he urged. "In fact, don't anyone move. We're going to be taking some more pictures."

At the look of concern on Alex's face, Cal put his goblet down so hard it almost broke the stem. This was the boys' first experience in a new setting. Telford was pushing things too fast. No one understood better than Cal that she didn't want the boys intimidated.

Her idea had its naissance after years of helping her mother set up these orphaned children with families, giving them the stability all children were entitled to. While they were at the park, she needed to be given space to work with them without drawing unnecessary attention to them.

Compelled to intercede, Cal stood up. "Sorry for the interruption, Bill, but I have to take Sergei outside. Before I leave, it occurred to me I'll be giving these volunteers a talk tomorrow evening. If you'd like, I'd be happy to take some pictures while they're at their campground—in natural surroundings."

"That's an excellent idea," Vance interjected. "Besides, the boys are probably tired after their flight from New Mexico today." The Chief's words meant he wasn't thrilled with Telford's zeal, either.

Without staying to hear Bill's response, Cal left the dining room with Sergei. It was difficult to keep walking when he knew Alex was right behind him. If the boys weren't with her, he would have asked her to leave the party and go to his house so they could talk.

He forced himself to keep on going and strode through the foyer to the entrance, needing the cold night air to brace him. A half hour later his phone rang while he was bringing the dog back to the house from their jaunt. It was Jeff. Cal clicked on. "I've been waiting for you to get home. Was my leaving like that too obvious?"

"Let's just say it silenced Telford for the moment. I sensed he didn't like being outmaneuvered, which leads me to believe he's personally interested in Alex. Vance was quick to protect her."

Cal had been aware of that, too. "So you've already talked to the Chief?"

"We just got off the phone. He's going to tell Bill to cool it for a while until the boys get used to being here. Vance is phoning Alex tonight so she won't worry."

"That's good."

"Judging by the way she left the dining room so fast, his call should come as a big relief."

"Yup," Cal muttered. "I'm glad the banquet's over."

"I guess we can consider ourselves official now. Catch you later. I don't know about you, but I'm bushed."

Cal hung up wishing he could say the same thing, but he felt wired. When he got back to the house, he'd phone his brother. Anything to get his mind off Alex, who was less than a mile away. All he had to do was get in his truck and he could be over there.

And then do what, Hollis?

In answer, all kinds of impossible images flashed through his mind.

FROM THE SUBLIME TO the ridiculous. Well, maybe not ridiculous, Alex amended on Sunday morning. But after a night at the Ahwahnee with its stained-glass windows and tapestries, the two-story ski retreat at Sugar Pines with its camp cots and simple bathroom and shower facilities would give the guys a new experience in semi roughing it. Girls on the top floor, boys on the main. Seventy in all.

The forest service staff had designated two big rooms for the H & H volunteers. Eight male teens to a room. The other large rooms were taken up by the male volunteers of the LTSY group. The smaller rooms housed the five chaperones and the director of the facility, Sheila Lopez, who'd been at the job close to a decade. Alex estimated she was in her forties.

A fireplace dominated the furnished common room. Alex was glad to discover the lodge didn't include television. The kids were expected to get out in nature and take advantage of all the talks and programs offered.

A cook and several assistants had been hired to live in and fix the meals in the spacious kitchen and dining area. With a staff that came in to do laundry and clean, the teens would be well taken care of.

After the boys had eaten a big breakfast that morning, Alex checked them out of the Ahwahnee and drove them in the bus to Sugar Pines only two and half miles away. Besides the lodge tucked up in the pines, there was a clearing with an amphitheater where you could view Half Dome.

The pueblo had its own earthy beauty, but she watched the guys' dark eyes light up as they explored their fabulous new environment. The videos she'd shown them could never compare to seeing the real thing. *God's front yard* summed it up to perfection.

If only Cal knew, he was her idea of perfection in male form. Perfect and unattainable, but he'd done her a favor last night. The teens appreciated the personal interaction when he'd shaken hands with them and tried to learn their names. They'd especially enjoyed Sergei.

The one thing they didn't like was having their pictures taken because it made them feel like they were something of a sideshow. Alex hated it, too. While they were at Yosemite, she wanted them to integrate with the other volunteers and discover shared interests, not stand out for being different.

Bill Telford was a dynamic, attractive man who meant well, but his appointment from Washington, D.C., made him an eager beaver. She wondered how he'd handle it if he were suddenly thrust into a different culture, the object of curiosity. Without the tempering of understanding that Cal had shown it would be an isolating experience. Last night when he'd broken up the photo shoot in an offhand way, her admiration for his sensitivity had grown.

At the thought of seeing him in a few minutes, her cheeks grew hot. Cal, along with Ranger Sims, head of security, was coming to talk to the kids. They'd be followed by Bert Rodino from the California department of road and trail reparations, who'd be explaining their specific job for the park.

After dinner, Sheila had told them to put on their parkas and assemble outside. It was still light when Alex and Lonan gathered their group and found places to sit with the other chaperones, Del Reeves and Marshall Phelps.

So far none of the teens, who'd come from all over the country, had started mingling yet, but she was confident it would happen after they'd been working on the trails for a few days.

In the distance she saw some trucks pull up in the parking lot. Soon three men approached. Even without Sergei at his side, Cal would have stood out. His height and rugged male physique seemed part of the magnificent surroundings themselves.

Once Ranger Sims had explained the rules of conduct while the youth lived within the park's confines, he turned the presentation over to Cal, who introduced himself and Sergei. After giving the same information on the bears that he had at the volunteer leaders' orientation, he switched to another subject.

"We have mountain lions here, not wolves, but you might go all summer and never see one. They stay away. Contrary to what you might think, there are more attacks on humans by deer than by bears. All the deer in Yosemite have mulelike ears so they're called mule deer."

The audience laughed.

"While you're repairing the trails, you'll see them in or near the meadows, browsing or grazing. Though they're naturally timid, they've grown accustomed to seeing people, but don't be deceived by them.

"Even if they appear tame and approach you, they're a wild animal and will charge if cornered or threatened. Their hooves and antlers are sharp. Always leave them a wide area to walk away and, like all the other wildlife, especially the coyotes, never tempt them with food."

As always, Alex noticed that Cal held the attention of his audience.

"At night you'll hear the coyotes singing in a chorus of howls, barks and yodels. They're natural predators of field mice and squirrels, but have learned to beg from people. Don't feed them. We have over two thousand food storage lockers to help with the problem. Human food is harmful to them. If they get conditioned to seeking food from people, it makes them vulnerable to being hit by passing cars.

"Keep in mind the park is the home to golden eagles, bighorn sheep and several endangered species, namely the great gray owl and the peregrine falcon. All wildlife is precious down to the shrinking toad population. Treat everything in the park as sacred. Watch where you walk so you don't crush a tiny forest creature by accident.

"On a final note, Yosemite is home to two hundred and fifty documented species of birds. There are nine hundred species in the entire U.S., so you can imagine how vital it is that the park remains a safe sanctuary for so many. If you see any animal or bird in trouble, report it immediately to your supervisors. The staff here has two-way phones to alert my office. I predict that if you'll treat this amazing world you've come to with respect, you're going to have the greatest time of your life here."

His smile as he wound up his talk upended Alex's heart. While Bert Rodino took his turn to speak, she watched Cal and Sergei circle the group. If she didn't miss her guess, he was taking a few pictures, but the kids weren't aware. By the time he reached her side of the amphitheater, he'd put the camera away.

Out of the corner of her eye she saw Sergei try to walk over to her, but the leash prevented him from reaching her. Alex was touched by the dog's affection, yet knowing his master wouldn't appreciate it, she pretended she didn't notice the two of them in order not to encourage Sergei. No doubt Cal wished she and his dog had never met outside the Chief's office.

Once Bert Rodino ended his presentation, Sheila took over. "Before you kids go back to the lodge for the night, let's give a round of applause to the experts who've taken time out of their busy schedules to talk to you."

Alex joined in the clapping, then got to her feet. Cal and the other two men stood conversing a little way off. Forcing herself to stay focused, she turned her attention to the boys starting to walk with her in the darkness. "What do you think so far?" she asked in English, but Lusio responded in Shiwi.

"The other kids don't like us."

His comment didn't surprise her. "Maybe they think you don't like them. Give them a chance. The fact that you've all volunteered to come means you're willing to do something different with your lives."

It was critical that the boys' time here got off to a positive start.

"You heard Ranger Hollis," she continued. "You're going to end up having the greatest experience of your life here, but it won't just happen without some effort on your part. For one thing, if you want to converse in Shiwi, do it when you're alone in your rooms. Otherwise speak English."

Lonan and the others had caught up with her. "Alex is right. You guys heard Mr. Rodino. Tomorrow you'll each be assigned someone outside your group to work with throughout the day. If you're friendly, they will be, too."

"The trick is to get them talking about themselves," she added. "Everyone likes the chance to brag." That brought smiles to their faces.

"Can we use our cell phones tonight?"

She looked at Lokita. Like the other boys, he was anxious to call home. "Sure, but you know the rules. At eleven, Lonan will gather them and it'll be lights out. You'll have to fit in your showers, too. I'll be knocking on your doors at seven in the morning to get you up for breakfast."

They nodded and hurried inside the lodge ahead of her. As she was about to climb the steps, she heard a deep, familiar male voice behind her say her name. Pulse racing, she turned around. The only light came from inside, making a silhouette of Cal's tall, imposing figure.

Sergei didn't waste any time greeting her. "Hi ya, boy." She leaned over to scratch his head.

"I'd like to speak to you for a minute. If you need to do something more with the boys, I'll wait." Since she knew he'd didn't want anything to do with her on a personal basis, it meant he must be here on park business.

"Getting the guys to bed is Lonan's department. I take charge in the morning." She stiffened slightly. "What's on your mind?"

It was too dark to read the expression in his eyes, especially beneath his hat, but she had the feeling he held his body taut, as if he were on alert. If he was on edge because he had to deal with her, he would soon discover she was no threat. They'd already had that talk to get the past out of the way, but he was probably wondering if or when the old Alex would resurface.

"Chief Rossiter wasn't happy about last night."

"You're talking about the picture taking. I know. He assured me it won't happen again without my permission."

"The superintendent sometimes gets ahead of himself."

"It's all right. At least he's forward thinking and anxious to show off the park's social diversity."

"Except that it's not going to happen overnight at your expense, no matter how much he'd like things to be otherwise."

"That's good to hear."

Cal shifted his weight. "I took a few pictures tonight because I promised Bill, but they caught a cross section of the volunteers and none of them were of you."

No. They wouldn't be…. Alex was so unforgettable, Cal had gotten married almost as soon as she'd left the park. "Thank you."

"The Chief doesn't want you or the teens being concerned about that while you're here."

Taking a fortifying breath, she said, "I appreciate that." She couldn't understand why Cal continued to linger. It was making her more and more uncomfortable. "Please tell Vance that's a big relief and I'm very grateful."

In fact she'd tell him in person the next time she saw him. As for this polite conversation with Cal, it felt so stilted, she couldn't stand it another second. *End it now, Alex.*

"The kids enjoyed your talk. I'm hoping they take it to heart. Good night." She patted the dog's neck one more time. "See you around, Sergei."

A low doggie moan followed her up the steps and inside the lodge. She never looked back.

"Alex?"

She glanced over her shoulder at Ralph Thorn, one of the male chaperones for the LTSY groups. According to Sheila, the sandy-haired public school psychologist from Torrance, California, had worked here last year, too. He stood by one of the tables in the lounge near the fireplace. A single guy of twenty-nine, he was kind of cute, like a young Dennis Quaid from *The Parent Trap* film.

"Hi, Ralph."

"I've been waiting for you to come in. Have you ever played cribbage?"

"No."

"Would you care to join me and learn?"

Yes actually, she would. Anything to get her mind off Cal. "Let me check on the kids, then I'll be back. But I'm afraid you're going to find out I'm not good at card games. Someone once tried to teach me how to play bridge. It turned out to be a disaster."

He answered with a slight smile. "I don't mind. We've got all summer."

She had a mental image of Cal eagerly driving away from the ski lodge now that he'd accomplished his mission. The summer was going to be endless unless she filled it with other distractions.

"Don't cry later that you weren't warned," she told him.

Once she'd talked with the boys and freshened up, she walked back to the lounge and sat across the small table from Ralph.

For the next half hour he took pains to teach her the fundamentals. "I told you I'm bad at this."

His eyes teased her. "It doesn't matter. I'm having fun."

"That's because you know what you're doing." Ralph was nice. She wished she felt a little spark. Anything to tear Cal out of her heart, but as soon as she compared other men to him, he seemed more implanted than ever.

"I noticed you outside talking to the new chief biologist. Introducing a bear dog to the park makes him different from the man he replaced."

"Why do you say that?"

"Because the ranger before him said it wasn't the park's policy."

"You *know* about bear dogs?"

He shrugged. "I heard about some being used for an experiment up in Washington, so I asked Ranger Thomas."

Alex thought it a little strange he was that interested, but didn't pursue it. She could have told Ralph he was way off course. The former superintendent's objection to the program was the sole reason bear dogs hadn't been introduced. There were too many other needs at Yosemite labeled top priority, but now that Cal was the head, Alex guessed he'd probably bought Sergei with his own money.

"Is he someone important to you?"

"Who?"

"Ranger Hollis."

That was none of his business. He was the second guy to ask about Cal. Talk about insecurity.

"I would think he's important to everyone considering he's in charge of watching over the wildlife." That was how she needed to think about Cal if she were ever going to be cured.

"You know what I mean. His dog seemed very friendly with you. I wouldn't want to tread on any toes, if you catch my drift."

She supposed his response made sense if he was simply flirting with her. "The dog could smell the tacos we had for dinner. As for Ranger Hollis, he was conveying Chief Rossiter's promise to help my volunteers feel welcome here. It's not going to be easy when none of them has ever been away from the pueblo before. They're a long way from home among strangers."

He started putting the little pegs away. "I'll do my best to get the kids I'm in charge of to befriend your group."

"That would be wonderful."

"Saturday I'm taking my bunch on their first outing. Want to come?"

"I'd planned to do the same thing with mine, maybe to Tuolumne Meadows. It's my favorite place."

"Mine, too. I was just up there the other day, but I'm thinking Tenaya Lake might be a better choice for their first hike since it's an easy one. Why don't you bring your volunteers and join us? It'll give both groups a chance to break the ice away from work."

Break the ice was right. Alex had been up there before. At an elevation over eight thousand feet, the lake probably still had frozen spots in early June. But the scenery was magnificent. Afterward they could continue on the Tioga road to the Tioga Pass Resort to spend the night.

"That's a good suggestion. I'll plan on it. Thanks for the invite and the game, Ralph. Good night."

"See you in the morning."

After she got to her room, she phoned the Tioga Pass Resort at the eastern end of the park. The management told her their cabins would be open to the public by Saturday. Given that news, she made reservations for her group. It was perfect.

Once she parted company with Ralph's teens on Saturday evening, she would drive her boys to the resort for an overnighter. The café served excellent dinners. After a week of hard physical work, they'd want to sleep in Sunday morning, then enjoy a big breakfast before driving back through the park to the Yosemite Valley. The teens would have the rest of the day to visit the museum and visitor center and do whatever they felt like.

Bert Rodino indicated the boys would be working on the Four Mile Trail. It wasn't that far from Sugar Pines campground. She thought it was the best trail for seeing the Valley. No matter how tired the boys might get, the great views down into the meadows toward Sentinel Rock, El Capitan and Yosemite Falls would be well worth it.

She wanted them to love it here. She wanted them to make friends and catch a vision for their lives that would impact them through the years. She wanted so many things. But it was clear there was one thing she couldn't have...*one person*...

Ralph would never know what the mention of Cal had done to her. After she got ready for bed, she buried her face in the pillow until it was so wet she had to turn it over.

Chapter Six

It felt like six years instead of six days since Cal had watched Alex go inside the ski lodge at Sugar Pines after saying good-night to him.

What she did out of his sight shouldn't be bothering him, but it was a troubling new experience to know she was somewhere in the park. And face it, Hollis, *She's leaving you alone just as she promised.*

His mood restless, he staggered out of bed after another night of tossing and turning, and headed for the shower. Once he'd shaved and dressed, he made coffee before going into the den to check the rangers' reports. The one from the park's resident botanist was more urgent than the others.

The El Portal Administrative Site and Yosemite Valley in the Merced River Canyon are showing signs of yellow star thistle. I haven't checked the Tuolumne Meadows yet, but I imagine it has sprung up there again and along the Tioga Pass Road.

Cal had this Saturday off. Since he'd made plans to take Sergei up to the Meadows to practice tracking bear scat, he would look for evidence of the pervasive weed at the same time.

A few minutes later he loaded Sergei in the crate in the back of the truck and took off under a partly sunny sky. The great wet seemed to be over and warmer temperatures were on the rise.

When he neared the Sugar Pines campground, he slowed down and reached for his binoculars. Alex's distinctive H & H minibus wasn't in the parking area. Knowing she craved adventure, she'd probably taken the teens on one of her favorite hikes. That included a lot of territory. With a whole day ahead of her, she could be anywhere.

He pressed on the accelerator. To his chagrin he found himself searching for her bus every time he passed a parking area en route to Tuolumne Meadows. So far he hadn't spotted her.

When he reached his destination, he put a leash on the dog and they spent a whole afternoon tracking bear droppings, mostly filled with berries and insect remains. Fallen trees from the ravages of winter provided the hungry bears with a feast of wood wasps they'd scratch out of the hollows.

Sergei was proving to be a great hunter. "Good job!" Cal praised him over and over. At a nearby stream he let the dog drink his fill. On the way back to the truck, Cal stopped to examine the plant life near the road.

Sure enough the star thistle had started to proliferate. The yellow heads were on the verge of budding into flower. He took pictures and put in a marker before getting back in the truck. For another couple of hours he stopped every so often along the road, marking the areas needing attention.

By 8:00 p.m. he was tired and starving. The café at the Tioga Pass Resort served good pot roast and apple pie. He'd eat there before driving home.

When he eventually turned off the road, his adrenaline surged to see Alex's minibus parked in front of the historic building. This late at night she and the boys would be staying over in the cabins.

"I'll be right back," he told Sergei, who rested his head on his paws inside the crate.

Once he'd gotten a key from the desk for a cabin, he entered the café and his attention was drawn to a head of gleaming, slightly windblown blond hair. Alex sat at a corner table with her back toward him, talking to two of her boys, who didn't look very happy. From what Cal could tell, they were having an intense discussion. The other teens must have gone to their cabins.

Cal walked over to the crescent-shaped wood counter and ordered his meal, then strode toward Alex. He was incapable of staying away from her.

The teens saw him coming first. They must have alerted Alex because she turned her head. Her eyes widened when she saw who it was. "Cal—"

In front of the boys, his first name had slipped out unbidden. That pleased him no end. It meant she hadn't completely put their past out of her mind.

"Good evening, everyone."

One of the boys said hi. "Where's Sergei?"

"In his crate in the back of the truck." Without conscious thought he reached for a chair from an empty table and pulled it up to theirs before sitting down. "Will you please tell me your names again?"

"Lusio."

"Mika."

He switched his gaze to Alex. "If I'm interrupting something important, I'll eat at another table."

"You can eat with us," Lusio said before Alex could tell him otherwise. They were finishing their pie.

"Thank you."

Cal motioned the waitress to bring his food to the table. After he'd been served and had taken a few bites he said, "How has your first week gone?"

Mika gave Alex a covert glance before looking down. Neither teen was forthcoming.

"Good for everyone except these two, I'm afraid," Alex explained. "The volunteers they've been assigned to work with aren't very friendly."

Cal nodded. "I know how hard that can be. When I first started work with the forest service in Idaho, I had to live with two guys in a remote cabin while we fought forest fires. I don't think we spoke ten words to each other for the first two months. No matter how hard I tried, they weren't interested in getting along, let alone being my friend."

Lusio squinted at him. "Try being Zuni."

Cal said, "Try being a white dude from Ohio assigned to live with two Nez Perce Native Americans who figured I didn't know squat about squat. The fact they were right didn't help."

Both teens broke into laughter. Alex flashed him a broad smile that reached to the empty place inside him, filling him with warmth. Their eyes held. "Did you end up being friends?"

"The truth?"

She nodded.

"No. Some prejudice you can't fight. My supervisor assigned me to a different crew of Nez Perce. We got along fine." With that remark he finished his steak and moved on to his pie, devouring it in one go. When he looked up at the boys, they were still grinning.

"Tell you what, guys. If things don't get better for you in another few days, I've got an idea you might like, except that it will be hotter and harder work than you're doing now. Alex probably won't approve."

Their dark eyes brightened. "Is it firefighting?"

"I'd never let you," Alex declared.

Cal smiled. "Nothing so dangerous. Every year weeds sprout in the park that have to be manually destroyed because they soak up too much moisture and crowd out the native plants. Worse, they're toxic to horses. The one we worry about most is the yellow star thistle."

Mika nodded. "We get a weed like that at home and have to get rid of it before the seeds blow around and ruin crops."

"That's right," Alex chimed in. "It's called musk thistle and fills our pastures. My brothers and I have to get out there with the backhoes and chop it up before it starts to flower."

Every time she opened her mouth, Cal learned something new about her that peeled away his former assumptions about her being spoiled rotten and pampered. When he thought about it now, he realized the labels he'd pinned on her had been rather harsh...and undeserved.

Yes, she'd been aggressive at times, but he was beginning to wonder if his initial reaction to Alex had much more to do with the experience that had driven him to leave Ohio in the first place when his brother's bride-to-be had unexpectedly put the moves on him. Was it possible *that* was the reason why—

"Do you want us to help cut the star thistle?" Mika's question broke in on Cal's tortured thoughts.

"If you're interested," he responded. "It's already growing along the roadsides and in patches in Tuolumne Meadows. Next week we'll be kicking off weed warrior week, a time when volunteers with the Bureau of Land Management come to Yosemite to help get rid of it. Last year they put in close to two thousand hours."

"That's a lot of weed pulling," Alex commented.

"There's a lot to do. You two boys could be put on a team with some guys your own age and work up here for a while. One of the supervisors would pick you up, bring you back and provide your lunch."

The excitement on their faces needed no translation.

"That's a terrific idea," she blurted. Just then she sounded like the excitable Alex he'd thought had disappeared on him for good.

"Why don't you two sleep on it and we'll talk some more in the morning over breakfast."

Alex looked startled. Her gorgeous green eyes swerved to his. "You're staying here tonight?"

"That's right. I'm bushed and don't feel like driving back to the Valley this late."

He studied her upturned features. "What time do you plan on being up?"

His question seemed to catch her off guard. "I…told the boys they could sleep in and we'd assemble here for breakfast at nine after the big crush of tourists has gone."

"I like the way you think and I'm sure your volunteers do, too." He put some money on the table. "Is Lonan with you?"

"No. We switch days off to give each other a break."

Good. "Then come on. I'll walk you to your cabins and say good-night to the others."

Alex stood up but looked away, confused, before she and the boys started for the entrance. Cal brought up the rear, enjoying the view. She wore jeans and a coffee-brown cotton sweater tucked in at the waist. On anyone else her outfit wouldn't have been remarkable, but the way the clothes outlined her womanly shape made looking anywhere else impossible.

They walked around to the cabins in back. The teens slept four to a room. Alex knocked on each door. When one of the boys opened it, Cal stepped inside to have a little chat and see if he could do anything for them. They seemed happy to see him and asked a lot of questions. Since they all wished Sergei were with him, he promised that after breakfast he'd get his dog to do a few tricks.

Finally he found himself alone with Alex. "Where's your cabin?"

"It's the next one down."

Heaven help him, but he didn't want to say good-night. "I have to get Sergei and feed him before I turn in. Why don't you come with me? I guess I don't have to tell you he'll be overjoyed to see you."

IF RANGER HOLLIS WANTED her company, it must mean he needed to discuss this new project for the boys out of their hearing. "After the meal I've just eaten, I could use a walk."

They headed for the parking area. She tried not to brush against him, but twice their arms touched, sending prickles of awareness through her. Over a year ago he'd crushed her to his hard-muscled frame and kissed her until she could hardly breathe. It wasn't an experience she could forget no matter how hard she tried.

"What did you do with your group today?"

Cal had told Alex he wanted her experiment to succeed. She accepted that, but she wasn't used to this new kind of interest from him. In the past he had never tried to prolong conversations, but she had to remember they'd agreed to forget the past. Too bad she didn't know how to do that.

"When I was worrying out loud to one of the chaperones a few nights ago, he suggested we take the kids to Tenaya Lake in the hope they'd bond, so we did. For the most part it worked. We walked around and took in the glorious scenery, but as you heard from Lusio and Mika, there isn't going to be an instant fix for everyone."

When they reached the truck, Cal lowered the tailgate. After attaching the leash to Sergei, he put out his food and water, then he turned to her. "Which chaperone was that?"

"Ralph Thorn."

"The one with wheat-colored hair?"

"Trust an old farmer like you to describe it that way," she teased.

He chuckled. "How would you describe it?"

"I don't know. I haven't really thought about it." Except that wasn't exactly true. When Alex had first met Ralph, she'd found him quite appealing and fun, but his behavior at the lake had upset her. He'd gone off with one of the boys who'd been rude to Mika and Lusio. They didn't come back for several hours, leaving her alone with both groups without explanation. She couldn't understand it and planned to discuss it with Chief Rossiter.

"He was here last year," Cal muttered, more to himself than to her.

"That's what he told me. In fact he made the remark that you were different from the former chief biologist."

His lips twitched. "Well, I am a few years younger than Paul. I'm glad he noticed."

Alex laughed. "I don't think he meant that." Cal had such striking good looks, she imagined insecure guys had trouble being around him for fear of an unfavorable comparison.

"Then what do you think he *did* mean?" His eyes pinned hers, and the heat there sent an unbidden warmth through her own body.

"I think he was surprised you had Sergei with you."

"For some people, a dog can be intimidating."

"Not when he's with a federal park ranger! The boys say they feel safer knowing you take him everywhere."

"Does that go for you, too?"

His voice sounded husky just then. "I've always felt safe around you. If anything, I feel sorry for the bears you're training Sergei to frighten."

Even in the dark, his white smile was visible. Alex had trouble concentrating. "Did you know you're the reason I drove to Redding to get me a bear dog in the first place? You talked me into it."

That was the last admission she would have expected him to make. "Who? *Moi?*"

"I didn't know you speak French," he teased.

Alex was loving their conversation far too much. "I didn't stay there long enough to learn more than a couple of words."

"But long enough to buy a bottle of expensive Chardonnay. You left it along with the basket of fresh croissants Ranger Ness and I devoured."

Heat flooded her cheeks. Alex had left the tower so fast, she'd forgotten about the food she'd taken him. Thank heaven for the darkness. "I'm glad it didn't go to waste."

"Not at all, but I've been saving the wine. Maybe sometime you and I can find a free evening to enjoy a glass together."

What was going on with him? She didn't understand this kind of olive branch he seemed to be offering. Alex refused to take any of this banter seriously. Cal's charm was lethal, especially when he teased. But she had to remember he was good at flirting when it meant nothing.

"With a dog and sixteen teenagers, I don't think that's in the cards."

"Let me worry about that."

In the next instant Sergei had finished his food and made a beeline for her. Alex burst into gentle laughter when he circled her, tightening the leash around her legs. "I can't move! Is this a new trick you've taught him?"

Cal came closer, his smile making her slightly

breathless. "No. He thought this one up all on his own."

In an effort to hide her emotions, Alex leaned over to give Sergei a hug. "I think Ranger Hollis has been teaching you a few naughty tricks and then blaming you."

"After our agreement to bury the past, don't you think you can call me Cal?"

Since he'd arrived at the resort, a change had come over him, mystifying her. He walked around her, Sergei following, until she could step over the leash. Free at last, she lifted her head. "I do actually."

"Good." He put the dog dishes back in the bed of the truck. "Come for a little walk with us before we turn in."

She went along with him, curious to know what he was leading up to. They began their jaunt bordering the woods outside the cabins. Sergei went everywhere to investigate sounds and smells.

"Does anyone ever call you Alexis? I saw the name printed in the brochure."

Once again he'd reduced their conversation to the personal, making her wary. "Only my mother. Who calls you Calvin?" Two could play at this game.

"*My* mother."

That made her laugh, but she didn't buy this new side of him. It hurt too much. "So, Cal?" She played along with him. "Why don't you tell me what you wanted to say about Mika and Lusio before I go in? I really do need to get to bed shortly." There'd be no sleep for her tonight, but he didn't need to know that.

He stopped walking. Though it was dark, she could see the warmth in his eyes. "I realize how much you want the boys to love it here. Whether you believe me or not, I want that, too. More than you know."

His assertion rang true. "Your kindness to the boys has already won their friendship. They have a way of seeing into hearts. That's proof enough for me."

Silence followed before he asked, "Enough to consider me a friend?"

A friend? After what had transpired at the lookout tower? After he'd married another ranger Alex hadn't known anything about?

To view him like that meant erasing certain memories which had become a vital part of her. She couldn't do it. But it was critical he see that her pathetic girlhood infatuation was a thing of the past.

"Of course. You can never have enough good friends. Until you walked in the restaurant tonight, the boys were hurting so badly, they told me they wanted to go back to New Mexico in the morning."

"What happened today to make them so unhappy?" It was no idle question.

"A boy in Ralph's group named Steve wanted to climb above the lake, but no one else was interested except Lusio and Mika. When Steve realized they wanted to join him, he changed his mind. Ralph asked me to keep watch while he took Steve aside to talk to him about his bad manners. But the damage was already done. Your intervention tonight came at a critical moment for them and me. I won't ever forget that."

She heard his sharp intake of breath. "I sensed trouble the minute I saw the three of you huddled together."

"A Ranger Is Always Prepared. I know the motto, but you also have the rare instinct for being in the right place at the right time. I'm grateful you're willing to give the boys a second shot at enjoying a Yosemite summer."

"They deserve one." His deep voice resonated inside her. "Why don't we do this. After breakfast I'll ask them if they'd like to drive back to Sugar Pines with me. On the way I'll show them where they'll be working and explain what's involved. If they're enthusiastic, then I'll hook them up with a couple of Paiute teens who'll work well with them."

Having Cal on her side where the boys were concerned felt like something of a miracle. "I can't ask for more than that. Just so you know, Mika and Lusio, in fact all the boys, know how to handle four-wheel pickups and do manual weed eradication. They help out on the ranches where they live."

"Then they're going to be a real asset."

"I know they will. Thank you. I'll see you in the morning. No—" she put out her hands "—I can get back on my own. You finish your walk. Good night." Without lingering to play with Sergei, she hurried to her cabin.

Once the door was shut, she leaned against it. A Cal who'd wanted nothing to do with her over the past six years, but had returned her kiss with equal hunger, was easier to deal with than this new friendly Cal. She was out of answers where he was concerned.

But by the time she'd climbed under the covers, she'd worked it out. His history with Leeann wasn't over, even if she'd been gone a year. Her ghost lingered in the park everywhere he turned. Cal had lost her here at the Tioga Pass, and he was lonely, missing her.

He was outside somewhere with Sergei now, reliving

his pain, needing another woman to fill his emptiness. Any woman. Even Alex, the pariah.

After waking early the next morning, Alex made calls to the boys' families to let them know how things were going. Already the positive feedback from the parents made her day. None of the boys were complaining about going home yet.

At eight o'clock she vacated the cabin in jeans and a navy hoodie. Sun shone from a clear blue sky. The mountain scenery was incredibly beautiful. She walked out to stash her backpack in the minibus. On her way to the café she saw the boys standing beneath some trees with Cal. They were watching him put Sergei through more tricks. He could bow and play dead. Smart dog.

When she looked up, she received the full brunt of a pair of brilliant blue eyes. "Ah," he said. "Now that your leader is here, Sergei will demonstrate how to kiss."

A Cal Hollis who grinned at her like that could set every butterfly loose in her stomach. The morning sun highlighted the lines of his rugged features. The boys were smiling at him. His rapport with the teens was nothing short of extraordinary. They had no idea how lucky they were to be taken under his wing.

She moved closer and leaned down to rub her hands over the dog's fur. "You're my buddy, aren't you." Sergei licked her twice, much to the boys' amusement. When she looked beyond the pointy ears, she discovered Cal's gaze focused on her mouth.

Once upon a time a look like that would have reduced her legs to jelly. But she knew the reason for it now. Let some other woman give him comfort.

After patting Sergei's head, she walked inside the café

and ordered breakfast for the whole bunch, including Cal. A minute later he joined her at the counter without his dog.

"He's been fed and watered," Cal said, answering the question in her eyes. "But he doesn't like being crated."

"No living creature does."

"That's a fact, ma'am."

Some people hated confinement more than others. Cal had picked a job that ensured he could be outdoors as much as possible. Alex remembered a film she'd once seen on prison inmates. They all agreed the thing they missed most was the sky. Cal had the sky and the mountains, but she knew they weren't enough to ease his pain over Leeann.

"I put in your order."

His eyes drifted over her. "How did you know what I wanted?"

"We're all getting the same thing."

One brow lifted. "I like surprises."

No he didn't. Not from her. But they'd agreed to be friends. If she was going to honor their pax, she needed to proceed as if this were a new beginning. "That's easy for you to say because you've probably eaten here a hundred times or more."

"Guilty as charged."

She turned to find an empty table next to her group and almost ran into one of the volunteers she'd met in orientation—the annoying guy with the spiky black hair.

"Hi, Alex." His brown eyes assessed her with blatant

male interest. He repelled her. "In case you forgot, I'm Brock."

"Your name was on the tip of my tongue. Are you here to take pictures? It's the perfect day for it."

"That's what I thought when I got up this morning. How would you like to hike to Lembert Dome with me?"

"Thank you for asking, but I'm afraid I can't. I'm here with my group of volunteers."

He glanced at Cal, who was helping the waitress pass the breakfast plates around. "This is the second time I've seen you with Ranger Smoky over there. If you've got a thing going with him, tell me now."

Both he and Ralph seemed obsessed with Cal. Why? Again she was irritated by his aggressive nature. He lacked people skills. She couldn't understand how he'd been hired to help at a public campground.

"We don't. Coincidences happen. Now if you'll excuse me, my breakfast is waiting."

"Mind if I sit with you while I order mine?"

Now was not the time to make a scene. "Be my guest." She headed for the table where Cal was waiting for her. He watched them coming and got to his feet without giving away what he might be thinking.

"Ranger Hollis? This is Brock—you saw him last week in the conference room. He works at Crane Flat. I'm sorry but I don't remember your last name."

"Giolas."

Cal shook his hand. "Sit down, Brock. How's everything going at the campground?"

"I can't complain." After he took a seat, the waitress came to take his order.

Alex dug into her breakfast. Between bites of his, Cal asked more questions. "What brought you to Yosemite?"

"The scenery."

"Brock's a freelance photographer," Alex interjected. He seemed pleased she'd remembered.

"You'll never run out of subject matter here whether it's people or scenery," Cal commented.

After swallowing the last of her omelet, Alex looked over at the boys. They'd finished their food. She could tell they were anxious to get going.

"If you two will excuse me, the guys are ready to board the bus." She stood up. "It's been nice to see you again, Brock."

"You, too," he muttered.

She'd prepaid the bill. Without any more discussion, she walked out with the troops, who were carrying their backpacks. Alex couldn't get away from Brock fast enough. Cal must have read her mind because he didn't detain her. There was something about Brock's personality that put her off.

Once the boys had stashed their stuff and taken their seats, Alex opened her backpack and handed them their cell phones. "During the drive back, you can give your families a running commentary on anything you feel like."

A glance out the window revealed Lusio and Mika standing next to Cal's truck. She stepped off the bus and walked over to them. "Ranger Hollis will take you back to Sugar Pines. In case I'm out, give me a call when you arrive and I'll come and pick you up. Here are your cell phones."

While she was handing them over, she saw Brock leave the café and head for a white Nissan Sentra. As he drove off, Cal emerged from the café and walked toward them.

Lusio looked at her. "Is it okay to call him Cal? He told us to."

"When you're alone with him, of course." Cal couldn't have done anything to win their trust faster than treating them like a friend.

He walked up and opened the passenger door for them to climb in. "I promise I'll take good care of them," he said.

"They're lucky to be with you."

"Just now you looked like a mother seeing her kindergarteners off to school for the first time. Your bond with them is very touching, you know that?"

Alex had trouble swallowing. "They're so sweet and sensitive. I love them." Her voice trembled.

"It shows. Otherwise you couldn't have gotten a whole crowd of come to a wilderness park when they've never left home before."

"Thank you for being here for them, Cal." *Thank you, thank you.*

Several hours later the minibus arrived at the Curry Village area. Her group wanted to eat lunch there before they went exploring. Alex told them to have fun. After the bus emptied she was about to close the door when eight-year-old Nicky Rossiter ran up. Roberta Jarvis, four years older, was right behind him.

"Hi, Alex!" the children cried in unison.

"Well, hi, you two! What's going on?"

"We just had tacos for lunch."

"They're good here, huh." Both of them nodded. "Where are you headed?"

"Back to headquarters," Nicky answered. "Our dads are in a meeting."

"Where's your mom?"

"She's home napping while Parker's asleep."

"I'm sure she needs it. What about your mother, Roberta?"

"On Friday she flew to San Francisco to be with my grandparents. She'll be back tonight."

"Will you tell her I'd like my volunteers to meet her? They'll be fascinated to learn a little bit about archaeology while they're here."

"Sure. She'd love to do that. I'll tell her to call you."

"Thanks. I'm at the Sugar Pines ski lodge."

"I know."

Nicky was looking at her with eyes that implored. "Can we have a ride in your minibus?"

"I was just going to ask if you'd like that. Climb on board." They needed no urging. "Wherever you decide to sit, be sure to fasten your seat belts."

"We will."

"This is fun!" Nicky cried. "I always wanted to ride in one of these."

Alex smiled. She'd only had the bus a little over a week. "Do you want to go straight to headquarters, or shall I take you on a guided tour of the Valley first?"

"A tour! Make it last a long time—we always have to wait and wait for their meetings to be over."

"I always had to wait for my dad, too. Are you strapped in?"

"Yes!"

"Okay. But first I have to check in with your father."

She pressed the button she'd programmed to reach the Chief. When he didn't pick up, she left a voice mail that the children were with her and they'd be back in front of headquarters in about twenty minutes.

"All right!" She started driving, then pulled out the mike and switched it on. "Ladies and gentlemen? Welcome aboard the H & H Express. What's so fabulous about Yosemite? It's got dozens of incomparable meadows and more than a hundred lakes, plus waterfalls as tall as a two-hundred-story building, trees the size of rocket ships, mountains the size of—well, mountains! And even a few beaches. It's bigger than a handful of European countries and nearly the size of Rhode Island.

"Today we have two very important people with us. Nicky's father is the chief of the *whole* park, and Roberta's father is the assistant chief of the *whole* park. We'll be touring the Yosemite Valley, so sit back and enjoy!"

Nicky whooped it up. Roberta was equally excited but less vocal because she was older. Twenty minutes later Alex slowed to a stop in front of the park administration building.

"Hey! There's our dads!" Nicky lowered the window. "Hi, Daddy!"

"Hi, Dad!" Roberta called out.

The two men walked toward the bus. Alex opened the door. They climbed on board with a smile. Chase hugged his daughter. "Looks like you've been having a good time."

Roberta nodded. "It's Alex's day off. We asked her to take us on a tour."

"Yeah," Nicky cried, "and she knows more than the rangers! She said we have trees as big as rocket ships." His giggle was infectious.

Vance's eyes lit up in amusement. "That's why she's part of the team, son. Since I need to talk to her, why don't you walk home with Chase and Roberta? I'll come by for you in a few minutes."

"Okay. Thanks, Alex! That was fun! Can we do it again?"

"Certainly."

"You're nice, Alex. Thank you." Roberta hugged her before the three of them walked away.

"You're welcome!" she called after them.

The Chief took the first seat opposite her. "Thanks for the voice mail. I appreciated that. I guess you realize you made Nicky's day."

"Those children made mine. Nicky's priceless."

He chuckled. "Agreed. Now tell me how your volunteers are doing."

"Because of Ranger Hollis's intervention, better than I would have thought." For the next few minutes she explained about Lusio and Mika.

He nodded. "Cal's done the right thing. I'm glad to hear he's gotten involved. Anything else to report?"

"Yes. I intended to phone Beth in the morning and make an appointment with you."

"Since I'm right here, let's talk."

"I'm concerned about a couple of things. The new volunteer at Crane Flat named Brock Giolas doesn't seem to fit the usual profile of people who work here. He's a guy with an attitude. Abrasive, you know? The first thing he wanted to know was whether Ranger Hollis and

I were an item. He blurted the question right out. Talk about a turnoff—"

"If I'd been a single guy and met you, I might have asked the same question."

Alex smiled. "Except you have a different nature that appeals to people. Brock's bizarre to the point of being boorish. Mind you, this is just my impression, but I keep wondering how he got hired. I understand he's a freelance photographer from Las Vegas in his spare time. If I were a tourist in the park needing help, I'd shy away from him."

While she was talking, he made some notes on a little pad he carried in his pocket.

"What else?"

"Ralph Thorn is one of the chaperones at Sugar Pines who was here last summer. He suggested we take our groups up to Tenaya Lake yesterday, ostensibly to mingle." She explained about Lusio's and Mika's hurt feelings. "He asked me to watch the group while he went off with Steve Minor, the teen who'd made them feel so bad. I thought he'd only be gone a few minutes."

"How long did you have to wait?"

"Two and a half hours."

Vance frowned.

"After a half hour I started worrying that something bad had happened, so I phoned him, but his cell had been turned off."

"I don't like the sound of that."

"I wasn't too happy about it, either. For one thing, he left me alone to manage his thirty teens along with my group. If there'd been an emergency, I was the only adult in charge. We'd been out a long time and some of his teens wanted to get back to Sugar Pines because they were hungry. As I see it, Ralph broke one of the cardinal rules discussed in our orientation.

"For another, he didn't stick to the rule about never being alone with a minor. We have that same rule at Hearth and Home for the children's safety. I'm not accusing Ralph of anything, but if there were a problem of that sort, Steve would have been at his mercy."

"What did you do?" Vance asked.

"I was on the verge of phoning Ranger Sims for backup when they finally showed up. I asked Ralph why he didn't answer my call, and he said he'd lost his iPhone somewhere and they were looking for it. That's why they were gone so long." Alex could hear the censure in her voice.

"I'm afraid I didn't buy his explanation. A phone can be replaced. If he'd lost it, he should have come back to the spot where we were all waiting for him. He must have realized we'd be worried. He could have gone back to look for his phone after he went off duty. At that point I didn't ask more questions because I didn't want the kids to think I was interrogating him."

"Could you describe the area for me where they hiked?" Vance asked.

Alex gave him her best estimate.

"I'll ask Chase to investigate. He'll talk to Steve before he gives Ralph a warning. He'll be careful so it doesn't reflect on you."

She sighed in relief. "That's good."

"Anything else?"

Alex bit her lip. "It's probably nothing."

"Let me be the judge of that."

"The other night when Cal came to Sugar Pines with Ranger Sims to talk to the kids, Ralph made the comment that it hadn't been Ranger Thomas's policy to introduce bear dogs into the park. I guess I was surprised he'd given it that much thought. When I asked him about it, he said he'd heard some bear dogs had been used as an experiment in Washington State, but nothing had come of it. I don't know why, but I got the impression that for some reason, he has it in for Cal. He asked me if Ranger Hollis and I had something going on."

"That makes two volunteers who find you attractive."

"But neither one of them acts like a normal guy hoping for a date," she objected. "There's a big difference."

"Understood. Tell me what else you know about Ralph."

"From the little I've learned, he's a public school psychologist in Torrance during the rest of the year. The other two volunteers at Sugar Pines happened to mention that Ralph was a nice guy, but he mostly kept to himself last year. That's all I know so far."

Vance finished making notations before pocketing his pad. "This is exactly why I hired you. Where's Ralph now?"

"I'm not sure. When we separated at the lake yesterday, I went on with my group to Tioga Pass and haven't seen him since."

The chief's eyes gleamed. "Did your boys like it up there?"

"I *know* they did. They were all smiles when I pulled up to the resort last night."

Vance got to his feet, "Bert Rodino says they're

working out just fine and do their jobs without com-
plaint. They're a real asset and so are you, Alex." His
praise meant a lot. "Keep up the great work." He stepped
off the bus.

"Thanks for letting me come," she called after him.
He waved before she headed for Sugar Pines.

The whole time Alex had been talking with Vance,
she'd been thinking of Cal. For her peace of mind, it was
time for her to concentrate on something else.

Chapter Seven

Cal pulled into Sugar Pines campground at six with Lusio and Mika. It pleased him to see Alex's minibus in the parking area. Now he wouldn't have to hunt her down. "When you guys go inside, would you find Alex and ask her to come out to the truck?"

The boys thanked him before walking inside to get her. While he waited, he returned a phone call from Jack, but his brother wasn't available. As he was leaving a message, he saw Alex come out the door and head in his direction. Every step she took made his heart pound a little harder. He hung up and got out of the truck, elated to have a legitimate reason to seek her out.

"The boys said you wanted to see me. Have you decided they might not be equal to the task after all?" In the dark he couldn't see the color of her fabulous eyes, but he could tell they were anxious.

"If I'd thought that, I wouldn't have made the suggestion in the first place."

He sensed her hesitation before she said, "But there is something wrong."

"I could use your help right now."

"What do you mean?"

"Sergei cut his back left paw on a piece of broken glass at the side of the road."

"Oh, no—"

"I need to put in a few sutures. Naturally I can do it alone, but I thought if you came to my house and held his head, he'd deal with it better." *I know I will.* Cal was determined to talk to her.

She didn't hesitate. "Of course I'd be happy to help. Let me run inside and tell Lonan. I'll be right back."

He waited by the truck for her. If it hadn't been for the dog's accident, he knew in his gut she wouldn't have agreed to come with him tonight. Until he explained certain truths to her, he'd never make any headway with her.

Before long she'd rejoined him. Once he was behind the wheel, he thrust her a sideways glance. "Sergei has taken a strong liking to you."

"The feeling's mutual."

"I could be jealous, but since it's you, I'm not complaining."

"I'm honored," she quipped. "What was broken glass doing by the road?"

"It was part of a headlight, most likely broken by the fender of another car. The average tourist keeps driving and doesn't stop to consider what he's left behind."

She sighed. "One of the hazards of park traffic. Is the cut bleeding hard?"

"I had to put a tourniquet on him."

"Oh, the poor darling. That means it's deep."

"Sergei will survive."

"Thank goodness."

Cal had to admit her soft spot for animals and children

was an endearing trait. He was discovering Alex had a lot of those, but before she'd come to the park this year, he'd purposely chosen not to notice her good qualities.

After years of putting her off, he was now using any excuse to spend time with her. Tonight he had to face another truth. He'd never forgotten the taste and feel of her. In his arms, the girl had become a woman. She'd been so alive, it had taken his breath away. The problem was, he wanted to see if it would happen again.

"You're so quiet, Cal. Are you all right?"

No. Even if he'd deluded himself into thinking he was over Alex, he would still have wanted her when she came to the park the next time, and the next.

With clearer vision now, he realized she couldn't help having been born a male magnet. She was simply one of those women who didn't have to do anything to attract men. He pressed the remote on his truck visor and drove into his garage, aware of a growing unease at the idea of another man getting close to her.

The string of admirers was growing longer. Telford for one. Thorn for another. As for Brock, it had taken all the willpower Cal had not to tell that loser to back off.

"Cal? What's wrong?"

"Sorry, Alex. I guess I'm concerned about Sergei's wound. I think the kitchen table will be the best place to stitch him up." After shutting off the engine, he handed her the keys. "It's the brass-looking one. If you'll open the door, I'll carry him in."

She moved fast to do as he asked. "Do you have a clean sheet?" She turned from the open doorway. "I could put it over the table."

Cal had already climbed into the truck bed. "Good

thinking. You'll find one on a shelf in the closet down the hall to the bedrooms."

By the time he'd carried Sergei through the house, she'd raised one side of the table and had folded the sheet double over the top. She'd also brought some clean towels that she put on the counter.

"Hey, buddy. We're going to take care of you. Alex is here." Cal smiled to see his dog lick her hands as she helped support his head.

"You're going to be fine," she crooned to him. "Dr. Hollis is on the job."

Chuckling, Cal reached in the kitchen cupboard where he kept his medical supplies. He took out a tranquilizer pill and a pain pill, then reached in another cupboard for the peanut butter. After finding a spoon, he scooped out a glob and put the pills in it before handing it to Alex.

"If you'll feed him this, I'll get what I need." When he had everything ready, he washed his hands and put on sterile gloves.

"I love your dog. He makes a great patient."

"I agree."

"Mmm, you like this stuff, don't you," she crooned to the dog. "You're being so good and courageous. Yes, you are." She smoothed the top of his head with her hand. He licked the spoon clean, then licked her fingers while Cal performed the surgery. Sergei had to be in heaven with attention like that.

"All done. Now for some antibiotic spray." Cal could see that Sergei's eyes were heavy from the tranquilizer. "That took five stitches, buddy."

Alex kept talking to the dog. "Mean old piece of glass. Now that it's out, you'll have to be extra careful where you step. Do you know Cal has wrapped your leg better than a certified vet?"

"I like the sound of that."

"It's true," she assured him. "You would have made a wonderful vet or even a doctor."

"You think?"

"I *know*. Anyone with training can put in stitches, but it's your bedside manner that distinguishes you. You made a huge difference for Mika and Lusio today. I'm very grateful."

Alex—

"If you'll steady him for another minute, I'll bring a blanket and he can sleep in here tonight."

"Did you hear that?" The dog made little sounds as if he understood. Cal came right back and fixed a bed for him in the corner. Alex sat down on the edge of it. When he lowered the dog, she let his head rest against her leg. "There, Sergei. It's all over and you're going to be fine."

Cal filled the water bowl and put it near them. The dog took a few drinks, then plopped his head back on her shapely limb. Cal would sell his soul to trade places with Sergei. The day was coming soon when he knew he was going to do just that, but the timing wasn't right.

He put everything away and carried the sheet to the washing machine. When he walked back in the kitchen Alex said, "Whoa—did you feel that?"

"What?"

"A tremor."

His gaze shot to his drugged dog, who made a low moan and tried to lift his head. Cal hadn't felt anything. He looked around. Nothing in the kitchen had fallen.

"Stay where you are, Alex, in case there's more." He reached for his phone and called headquarters to report in. After a minute Chase came on the line.

"The quake's been felt everywhere, Cal. It was a magnitude three running through the Sierra Nevadas just outside the park about six miles south of Mammoth Lakes. The Mono County sheriff's dispatcher says there have been no reports of damage or injuries."

Alex eyed him with a concerned expression.

"None at my house, either. Do you need me?"

"Not yet. For the moment we've got things covered. I'll wait to get back to you until after the rest of the reports come in. If you don't hear from me, then don't worry about it."

"Any news from Sugar Pines?"

"No.

"I'll call over there."

He hung up and looked at Alex. "Do you have Lonan's number programmed?" She nodded. "Give me your phone."

She pulled it out of her jeans pocket. "Press two."

Lonan was quick to answer. Cal identified himself. "Are you all right?" He put the speaker on so she could hear.

"Everyone's fine. We're outside listening to a talk by the park historian. Some of the kids felt a vibration, but not everyone. No problems."

"Thank goodness," Alex whispered.

"That's the way it happens."

"Sheila wants us to wait out here. She'll tell us when it's safe to go inside."

"Good. She knows what she's doing. I'll bring Alex by later."

"No hurry. How's the dog?"

"His operation was a success."

"The kids were a lot more concerned about the dog than the earthquake. Now they'll be able to settle down."

A smile broke out on Alex's face, erasing her worry lines.

"Lokita's been complaining of stomach pains again, but he refuses to do anything about it. I think he should go over to the clinic."

"He gets those every once in a while," Alex interjected. "He might have an ulcer. Let's cut out all spicy food for him. If it doesn't subside by morning, I'll take him to the clinic. Talk to you later, Lonan."

Cal gave her back the phone. "Except for Lokita, so far, so good, but we'll just sit tight until I hear from Chase."

"I think you-know-who is going to sleep fast."

The combination of medicines had started to work. He nodded. "I'll take a minute to run in the den and see if any of my staff has tried to contact me."

"Go ahead. We'll be fine."

She looked so adorable sitting there with his dog, he had to suppress the urge to get down on the floor with her. The tremors shaking his body had nothing to do with the quake.

"You make an excellent nurse," he said on his way out of the kitchen.

"Thanks, Doctor."

ALEX GLANCED AT SERGEI. He was down for the count. It felt a little cool next to the floor. She reached for one of the bath towels and laid it over him.

When Cal came back in the kitchen, she glanced at him. "I don't think he'll wake up," she said in a quiet voice. "Would you mind driving me back to camp? I want to check on the boys. If any of their families heard about the quake on the news, I'd like to reassure them before the night's out."

"Don't worry," he said in a low voice. "Lonan will already have done that. We can't leave yet. Chase told me to stay put."

"Did he give you any reports of injuries or damage?" When Cal didn't say anything, she asked, "Any rock slides from the tremor?"

"None. The park got off lucky this time." His words sounded remote.

"I'm glad of that for everyone's sake. Luckily Sergei didn't seem to be frightened."

"No. In any case, he was too drowsy." Cal sounded far away. She wondered if the earthquake had brought back memories of his wife's death in one of those natural disasters that struck the park on occasion.

She watched in surprise as he went to the cupboard and got down two glasses and the wine she'd brought him. After popping the cork, he poured a small amount into each one and handed her a glass. "I thought this would be the perfect time to drink to new beginnings." A change had come over Cal.

"To the new chief biologist," she purposely declared. Their fingers touched, igniting her longing for him despite her determination not to let him affect her. She drank it quickly. "That tasted good."

After draining his glass, he reached for her empty one and put both on the counter. Then he stared at her. "I was referring to *us*." The huskiness in his voice raised the heat in her body.

She had to say something to stop the uncertain thudding of her heart. "You mean my volunteer job. I guess in that regard we've both achieved something we've wanted for a long time."

She couldn't imagine what was on his mind. For all she knew Vance had given Cal a secret job like he'd given Alex—one no one else knew about. While she'd been asked to spy for the Chief, Vance might have asked Cal to help ex-senator Harcourt's daughter make a success of her project with the boys.

It was all in the interest of the park, but the possibility that Vance could have put Cal up to this felt like another body blow. After learning Cal had been married when she'd come to the park last year, Alex couldn't stand any more hurts.

Cal sat down on one of the chairs with his elbows on his knees, hands clasped in front of him. "We may have done that, but I'm talking about us personally. While we're waiting to hear from Chase, there's something important I want to talk to you about."

Like the seismic activity beneath the earth, there'd been a shift in her dealings with Cal. They'd never had a relationship and you could hardly call it one now. She no longer lived in a fantasy world where he was concerned. Her parents would be relieved to know that, much as she might find Cal the most desirable man alive, she'd discovered that she'd never been even a blip on the screen of his life.

Those honors had gone to Leeann. It took two hands to clap. All along she'd tried clapping with only one. No wonder there'd been no sound, but she'd been a late bloomer and a slow learner...until now.

"What did you need to talk to me about?" Being in his house now didn't seem quite real, not after all the years she'd hoped in vain for the slightest sign he wanted her company.

"I owe you an apology."

That surprised her. "Apology? For what?"

"For some of my preconceived notions about you."

"You mean about my being the willful, spoiled rotten, pampered, empty-headed blond daughter of the senator from New Mexico that you got stuck with whenever the Chief asked you to show my father around? It was the truth."

"No...it wasn't. That's what I'm trying to say."

"Cal, we've been over this ground already."

"Not the ground I want to talk about," he asserted. "Did I ever tell you why I became a ranger?"

His question threw her—he'd never confided in her before. "As I recall, you said something about being tired of never seeing anything but flat horizon everywhere you looked from the farmhouse window."

"I'm afraid that was a lie," he confessed, surprising her further. "I loved the farm. Growing up I couldn't have imagined living anywhere else. I loved my family, my three brothers, especially my older brother, Jack. He was my idol. But a terrible thing happened the night before he got married, forcing me to leave home."

Why was he telling her this?

"It was the night before Cincinnati's wedding of the year—merging two prominent families. When I pulled into the garage, his fiancée, Helen, was there. She'd been the high school beauty queen and was probably the most spoiled, headstrong female I'd ever known, but Jack had loved her forever.

"I assumed she was waiting for him and told her he and my brothers were still at the hotel celebrating. As I was getting out of the car, she made her move and came on to me. She'd been drinking and threw her arms around my neck.

"At first I thought it was some kind of joke, but when she tried kissing me and told me I was the brother she'd always had the hots for, I was so repulsed, I pushed her away and went in the house where I threw up."

Alex had already put two and two together and didn't want to listen to any more. Carefully removing Sergei's head from her leg so she wouldn't wake him up, she got to her feet and started for the doorway, but felt Cal's hands on her shoulders. She couldn't stand for him to touch her now.

"I knew this would be your reaction, Alex," he murmured into her hair. "But you're not leaving until you hear the rest, so you'll understand."

She eased out of his arms to face him. "It's okay, Cal. I get the picture. The lookout tower must have been déjà vu for you. Wrong woman, wrong man. Enough said. I'll call Lonan to pick me up at headquarters so you won't have to leave Sergei."

His eyes roamed over her features. "I'm not through yet."

"But I *am*. Does that mean anything to you?"

Lines of strain bracketed his mouth. "If it's what you want, I'll take you back now, but one day soon I intend for you to hear the rest."

Not if she had anything to say about it.

Once they were in the truck, he opened the garage door with the remote. She felt his covert glance on her. Before long they reached the Sugar Pines parking area. To her surprise there were some kids still outside, but it looked like they were starting to file into the lodge. "Isn't that Bill Telford's Dodge power wagon?"

"So it is."

She frowned. "I hope nothing's wrong."

Cal pulled to a stop. "Let's find out, shall we?"

She jumped down before he could come around to help her and hurried toward the adults standing together.

"There you are, Alex." The superintendent stepped away from the group of chaperones to greet her. She noticed Ralph wasn't among them.

"Hi, Bill. Is there a problem here?"

"No, no. I told Vance I'd drive over to reassure the volunteers. It provided me with an excellent opportunity to talk about park safety. I wanted to be on hand to answer any of their questions."

"Were there a lot?"

"Yes. It made an interesting evening."

She smiled. "I hope they realize how privileged they were to have access to the *superintendon,* as Nicky Rossiter used to call you."

He threw back his head and laughed. "The park wouldn't be the same without that little guy."

"With a dad like Vance, he'll make some kind of a ranger one day."

"You can say that again." As he studied her, the mirth left his eyes to be replaced by a more serious look. "I was hoping to find you here earlier, but it appears you and Ranger Hollis were otherwise occupied."

His gaze flicked to Cal, who stood a few feet apart from her in what she considered his on-alert stance—all that muscle and sinew tensed, ready for action. Cal wasn't thrilled by the way their conversation had ended, but as far as she was concerned, there was no reason for a personal discussion ever again.

"I commandeered Alex to help me," Cal explained at last.

She couldn't understand why he wasn't more forthcoming. "Sergei got a deep cut in his paw from a jagged piece of glass."

"So the boys were telling me. That's not good."

"He needed emergency treatment," Alex told him. "I helped hold the dog while Cal put in some stitches. That's when we felt the tremor. I'm thankful everyone's safe."

Bill let out a sigh. "We'll all sleep better tonight knowing that."

Considering his heavy responsibility as government steward over the park, no doubt he *was* relieved, but Alex sensed an odd tension between him and Cal. It made her feel uneasy. "If you'll both excuse me, I'm going to check on the boys and phone a few parents who might have heard about the quake."

"I believe Lonan already took care of that, Alex. Before I leave, I wanted you to know I'd like to see you in my office next Friday. Let's say noon. We'll make it a working lunch while we talk."

He'd been looking at her while he spoke and hadn't included Cal in the invitation. She didn't know what to think, but she couldn't ignore a summons from the superintendent. "I'll be there. Good night, Bill."

Her glance included both men before she hurried inside the lodge, anxious to separate herself from Cal. After what he'd just told her back at his house, she had no desire to be alone with him again. His confession had dredged up all the pain of the past year in an agonizing new way. She was through with this kind of torture.

"Wait up, Alex…" Jerked out of her troubled thoughts, she saw Ralph headed toward her. "Where were you? Don't you know you missed all the excitement?"

After her talk with Vance, she had to be careful not to let Ralph know she'd voiced her complaints about him. They had the rest of the summer to get through. Somehow she needed to remain friendly, but from now on she would be wary about depending on him unless it was absolutely necessary.

Though he pretended a personal interest in her, she was positive it had nothing to do with his being attracted to her. He would have seen Lusio and Mika with Cal earlier. She had a feeling he'd noticed her return with Cal a few minutes ago and was fishing for information about him. Why, she couldn't say. The man had an agenda and she guessed it had to do with Cal. If she played along with him, maybe she'd discover what it was.

"Did you hear that Sergei cut his foot?"

His lips tightened. "Someone mentioned it."

"That's where I was, holding the dog while Ranger

Hollis sutured his wound. During the operation we felt the tremor. I hurried back as soon as I could. Are your kids okay?"

"A few got nervous, but they're fine now."

"That's good. I need to check on mine."

"Before you do that, I thought we should plan another outing for next Saturday. Most of the teens got along pretty well yesterday."

"But not all," she reminded him.

"I told Steve he had to apologize to the boys. He's done that already, so we'll hope for no more fireworks."

"I'm glad he did that. What do you have in mind?"

"A trip to the Hetch Hetchy Valley. We could do the Lookout Point Loop."

Alex had been there many times. The place looked like a replica of the Yosemite Valley. Bears and rattlers were common. According to Chief Sam Dick, the Paiutes once dug for acorns that had fallen at the base of the valley's black oaks.

"That's one of my favorite places. Sounds good. Let's talk about it during the week."

"How about tomorrow evening over another game of cribbage?" His eyes looked hopeful. He was attractive in his own way, but it was too bad she couldn't trust his motives.

"You're on. See you in the morning at breakfast."

Alex left him to find Lonan. He would want to go on that trip, too. She needed him there for backup in case anything went wrong. They could eat breakfast at the Evergreen Hotel first.

She'd ask Vance if he could arrange for Chief Sam Dick to talk to the kids before they started their hike.

Considering their Zuni background, he would enchant them with stories of his Paiute heritage. The blending of their two cultures would be an enriching experience.

Lonan answered the knock on his door. "Welcome back."

"This has been quite a night. Are you okay?"

"Sure. Everything's fine."

"I'm sorry I wasn't here."

"The boys agreed the dog was more important."

Alex nodded. "Sergei is very special to Ranger Hollis."

"And Ranger Hollis is very special to you."

That was true. She and Lonan had few secrets. They'd been friends since she was a little girl and pretty well knew each other inside and out. The two of them reminded her of Nicky and Roberta, who were also four years apart, but their bond was strong.

"Did you phone Mankanita?" Alex planned to pay him a big enough salary that he'd be able to marry Mankanita in the fall, knowing he had a nest egg in the bank.

"Yes."

"I bet she was happy to hear from you."

His dark eyes glinted with light. "She let everyone know about the quake."

"That's a relief. I didn't want anyone to worry. The next time you talk to her, why don't you invite her to come up next weekend and be with you while we visit the Hetch Hetchy Valley. I'll pay for her airline ticket and a rental car. She can room with me. I think she's missing you too much."

A happy smile broke out on his face. "She might be able to come. I'll ask her."

"Good."

"One more thing. Lusio and Mika phoned their parents and told them they want to become park rangers."

"What? They've only been here ten days! Yesterday they wanted to go home."

"Things change."

That was because of Cal, of course.

"Get a good sleep, Lonan."

"You, too."

Chapter Eight

By Friday Sergei's bandage had come off and he barely favored his hind paw. When Cal spoke with Gretchen about the injury, she said another week and his dog would be good as new and able to do deep-forest bear tracking. For this week, she recommended short walks.

Under the circumstances Cal didn't mind. With Weed Warrior Week here, he decided he would drive Mika and Lusio to and from the Tuolumne Meadows, while he carried out his own duties at the same time.

But he couldn't lie to himself any longer. Today was Alex's meeting with Telford and it was eating him alive. Cal had inside information from Jeff. Someone on the superintendent's staff had told him Telford was interested in Senator Harcourt's sexy daughter.

After four days of not seeing her, the need to make contact was so strong, Cal found himself driving over to Sugar Pines at 6:30 a.m. The other night she'd refused to let him finish explaining what was on his mind. This morning nothing could keep him from her. Somehow he would make her listen, hopefully before she took off to deliver her teens to their work site.

When he arrived, the kids were still eating breakfast.

He waited in the truck until he saw her file out of the lodge with the other chaperones and head for her mini-bus. Alex had dressed in jeans that outlined her shapely hips and long legs. She wore a khaki blouse tucked in at the waist, giving her an hourglass figure.

If she walked into Telford's office looking like that, she'd give him a heart attack. Maybe that wouldn't be such a bad idea, Cal mused wryly.

He climbed down from the cab to intercept her. She slowed down. "Cal…" Her green eyes scrutinized him in the early light. He couldn't decipher what she was thinking.

"Good morning. I'm glad I caught you in time."

"Is there a problem?"

He put his hands on his hips. "Why do you always imagine the worst?"

An almost smile hovered at the corners of her mouth. "Bad habit, I guess."

"Since I have to go to Wawona this morning, I'm here to take Mika and Lusio with me. They can catch their ride to the Meadows from there." As if saying their names had conjured them up, the two boys came out the door of the lodge with the other kids.

She looked surprised. "After what they told Lonan about you, they'll be thrilled to drive with you."

"Is that so?"

"Yes. They've decided they want to be rangers when they grow up. That's your fault."

He was surprised at how happy that made him feel. "I'm glad someone around here appreciates me."

"They like the volunteers you assigned to work with them much better, too."

"And what about the job itself?"

"It's what they've done at home so they're fine with it."

"Except it might be a different story by the end of today. The weather has turned warmer. By afternoon the sun will be hot."

"They're used to heat. How's Sergei?"

"Recovering nicely. He's in the back of the truck in his crate. By now he's dying to bolt because he can hear your voice. Why don't I pick you up this evening after the kids have had dinner. I'll fix you something to eat at my house. Sergei has missed you and could use a visitor."

"I'd like to come, but one of the botanists has been scheduled to speak to the kids. I need to be here."

Cal wasn't about to take no for an answer. One way or another, he intended to be with her tonight. "Then I'll be by for you after it's over."

Her hesitation before answering made him uneasy. If she was nervous around him because she really didn't like him anymore but couldn't show it while working at the park, that was one thing. But if it signified she was fighting an awareness of him after promising to leave him alone, that was something else. Before too much longer he was determined to learn the truth.

"I'll have to check with Lonan. I don't know if he has plans or not."

Alex, Alex. How much damage have I caused?

"Let me know later." He flicked his gaze to Lusio and Mika. "Hey, guys? I'm your ride this morning. Hop in the truck."

Their faces broke into smiles. At least *they* seemed happy to see him.

"MR. TELFORD? YOUR ASSISTANT told me to knock."

When the superintendent saw Alex in the doorway, he left his desk to walk over to her. "What happened to Bill? That is my name."

"I didn't think you would want me to be informal in front of your staff."

"Well, I do. Come in." His office had a coffee table with love seats facing each other. "Please…sit down."

"Thank you."

He sat opposite her and leaned forward with his hands clasped. "If you're thinking I asked you here to talk about your project, you'd be wrong. Vance told me to give your volunteers some space and I thoroughly understand. Forgive me for getting too excited about it?"

She warmed to him. "There's nothing to forgive."

"Thank you, Alex." His brown eyes studied her. "As you know, I don't have a big staff here. The person I rely on most is my assistant, Melanie Sharp, whom I brought with me from D.C. when I accepted the park appointment. She's been with me eight years. Now it seems I'm going to lose her because she's getting married and moving back to Virginia."

"I'm sorry for you. When dad lost his D.C. assistant, it took a long time to find the right replacement."

"I knew you'd understand. Once you've learned to rely on someone, you get spoiled. Trying to find a new one is like going out on a first date."

Alex couldn't help laughing. "I've had a few of those myself and know what you mean."

"I've done a bit of it since my wife died and it's not pretty."

Alex was seeing him in a different light, one she liked.

"I'm sorry you lost your wife. I can't imagine how hard it's been for you to carry on."

"You don't really have a choice. Lucky for me I have two children and a job I love. My only big problem at the moment is putting the right person behind the desk in the next room. What are your plans after your boys return to New Mexico?"

"What I've been doing for years, which is working for Hearth and Home in my spare time."

"Is there a man you're interested in at home?"

"No." Much as she cared for Lyle Richins, she knew it wasn't love and that was never going to change.

"The reason I ask is because I'm wondering if you would consider coming to work for me. You're just the sort of woman I'm looking for, someone who lights her own fires."

So this was what he'd been leading up to. Until a year ago she would have leaped at such an offer, but there'd been a dramatic change in her life and the answer had to be no. The park wasn't big enough to hold her and Cal.

"I'm very flattered you would even consider me, Bill. It's a real honor."

"But…" he responded with a sad smile. "I can hear it coming."

"I'm afraid the answer has to be no, and not because of a man at home. The truth is, I'm still trying to figure out my life. In order to work for you, I'd want to be a thousand percent committed."

He nodded. "I understand, but I have to tell you I'm disappointed. When I couldn't get you to stay at dinner the other night at the Ahwahnee so I could ask you, I had to do something else."

"You mean you *planned* for our tables to be close together…to talk to me?"

"Yes. And the picture taking was one way I could think of to detain you, but you left anyway."

"I had no idea."

"I've been so impressed with what you've done, I decided to try to nab you before you get some notion to become a ranger yourself."

She shook her head. "No. That would never happen. I've loved my freedom to play tourist here." After this summer Alex doubted she'd ever come to the park again. It would be too painful.

He sat back against the cushion. "You'd make a terrific one. Vance has said the same thing."

"You're both very kind."

"We both know a good thing when we see it." He smiled. "Thank you for being frank with me about the job. I had to ask. With that settled, let's walk over to the Yosemite Lodge. Our lunch is waiting. I'm anxious to hear an off-the-record account of how your volunteers feel about their experience so far. If there's anything they need, all you have to do is ask."

Touched by his concern, Alex willingly followed him out the door. As they rounded the corner she caught a glimpse of Cal striding down the hall. Sergei wasn't with him. She couldn't tell if he saw the two of them, but even from the distance separating them, his face looked hard as Yosemite granite before he disappeared inside his own office.

SINCE GETTING BACK FROM Wawona, Cal had a ton of paperwork to wade through. But after an hour he couldn't concentrate any longer and checked his watch. Alex and Telford ought to have finished their lunch by now.

As far as Cal was concerned, the superintendent was poaching on his territory, and to be on the lookout for poachers was the job of every ranger. *Unless* Alex had a thing for him. Cal couldn't imagine her being interested in a fifty-year-old man with children only a couple of years younger than her. The very thought chewed him up inside.

He pushed himself away from the desk. "Come on, buddy. It's time for an intervention, whether she likes it or not." After attaching the leash to Sergei, they walked out to the truck. No longer needing to be in a crate, the dog climbed into the front of the cab with him.

With a firm plan in mind, he drove to his house and exchanged the truck for his blue Xterra. He put Sergei in the backseat, then drove by the Yosemite Lodge parking lot. Her minibus was no longer there. Operating on the hunch she would go back to the ski lodge before she did anything else, he headed for Sugar Pines.

His heart slammed into his ribs when he pulled into the campground and saw her getting out of the bus. The angle of the sun bathed her hair in silvery-gold fire. Cal had never seen anything like it.

He got out of the car at the same moment Ralph Thorn bounded out of the lodge and hurried toward Alex. Evidently she couldn't go anywhere without a man lying in wait for her. It was no accident that Brock whatever-his-name-was had shown up at the Tioga resort last weekend.

Cal approached them, nodding to Thorn, who saw him first. In the other man's eyes there was a veiled glint of hostility before he recovered. It was one thing for the chaperone to show impatience at being interrupted while he was talking to Alex, but hostility connoted something else. Thorn had come to the wrong place to work if he had issues with the rangers, or Cal in particular.

"Good afternoon."

At the sound of his voice, Alex swung around. In that instant he glimpsed surprise in her eyes and another emotion that might have been relief. That made him more curious than ever.

"I need to speak to you, Ms. Harcourt. It won't take long. When you have a moment, just step over to the car."

He walked back and made a call to one of his staff, leaning against the passenger door. Pleased when she broke off talking to Thorn and hurried toward him, he hung up.

"Is there something wrong with the boys?"

Cal wasn't surprised that was the first question to come out of her mouth. She had a habit of worrying about them, but in this case it gave him an opening he would use to his advantage.

"To my knowledge everyone's fine. I'm off to do my afternoon rounds. This will be Sergei's first outing without being in his crate. If you'd like to see Mika and Lusio in action before I bring them back to camp, come with us. I thought we'd go in comfort."

Though he felt her hesitation, the unmistakable light in those green orbs told him she'd love the opportunity to visit them.

"They may not be demonstrative, but like any young guys, they'll enjoy showing off in front of you."

He could hear her mind working. "I'll take some pictures of them and Sergei to send home to their families. Give me a minute to run inside first."

She was still wearing the same outfit he'd seen her in that morning. It meant she hadn't felt the need to dress up for Telford. That, plus her eagerness to join him—even if it was tied to her affection for the boys and Sergei—improved his mood. Before the day was out, he would finish the talk with her that should have happened years ago.

In another few minutes she returned. No sign of Thorn. "Do you want me to sit in back with Sergei and hold him?"

Cal had a feeling that was what she preferred to do, but he was ready for her and held the passenger door open. "He's no longer an invalid, but I think he'd better have the whole seat to himself to rest his paw. To be honest, I'd like your company up front. It'll be nice not to have to crank my neck every time I want to look at you."

"All right" came the quiet response.

Their arms brushed as she got in. Her long, jeans-clad legs drew his attention before he closed the door and went around to the driver's seat. She got on her knees and reached over the seat to pet the dog. "How's my little sweetie?"

Sergei went into ecstasy. When she turned to smile at Cal, he felt breathless. "I think you already have your answer."

"I'm so glad he's getting better." She finally turned around and fastened her seat belt.

"He is, too."

Wishing he could take off and be alone with her for weeks on end, Cal started the car and had to be satisfied that for the rest of the day he'd know exactly where she was and what she was doing. He had no idea what the evening would bring, but he'd work that out later.

En route he caught the nod of a ranger here and there. He understood their double takes when they saw Alex in the car with him. Speculation would be rife because Cal hadn't been with another woman since Leeann.

Not only that, Alex would have been spotted earlier eating lunch with Telford. Hopefully the superintendent would learn she'd gone straight from lunch to spend the afternoon with Cal. His colleagues were going to have to get used to it.

He flicked her a glance. "What do you have planned for the boys this weekend?"

"Ralph suggested we go to the Hetch Hetchy Valley in the morning." Thorn again. "I spoke with Vance and he's arranged for Chief Sam Dick to talk to the volunteers tomorrow after we reach the campground."

"That's a real honor."

"I know. My boys especially will relate to him in a way the others can't."

She was right. "Are all the groups going?"

"I think everyone will come."

"Will you be going back to Sugar Pines after?"

"No. My boys will be staying over at the Evergreen Lodge."

Cal had to attend an all-day seminar in Bishop tomorrow with some national forest service heads. He wouldn't get back until late. Possibly too late to join her.

"The boys are going to have a fantastic opportunity."

She nodded. "Lonan's fiancée, Mankanita, will be arriving later today for the weekend. I wanted her to meet Chief Sam Dick and his wife. If this experiment works out, maybe she and Lonan will come next summer and bring some of the girls. too."

"Lonan's a good man."

"Mankanita's a wonderful woman. If she approves of what she sees, it will carry a lot of weight with the tribal council for the future."

He looked over at her. "Without you, none of this would have been possible."

"Don't give me any credit. It's all because of great-great-grandfather Trent. If he'd seen Yosemite first…"

"He and John Muir. That would have been quite a meeting."

"My ancestor would have immediately claimed all the Yosemite Valley for himself and El Capitan would be named Mt. Silas."

Cal threw back his head and laughed. "I'll never forget my first sight of the Falls and Half Dome. I'd just been transferred in from Rocky Mountain Park. It was beautiful, but nothing compared to the topography of Yosemite." He paused for a minute before he added, "If it hadn't been for Helen, I would have missed the whole experience."

With those words, he felt Alex retreat, but he didn't care because it had to be said.

"I'll never be sorry for what she did, Alex. That was the night the world as I knew it changed for the better for me. I packed my things and left after their ceremony was over. It didn't matter where I went. I just wanted to get far away for a while and ended up in Idaho."

"Why there?"

So she *was* listening.

"Idahoans buy a lot of Hollis Farm Implements. On a whim I booked a flight to Coeur d'Alene to see what it was like before I flew on. It just so happened there was a huge forest fire blazing. I mean gigantic. The flight had to be diverted to Spokane, Washington.

"From there I rented a car and drove to Coeur d'Alene, curious to view it up close. When I saw the lines of fire-fighters flown in from all over, working together against nature, it ignited something in me. I hired on there with the forest service. Months later one of the men I worked with said that if I loved the mountains so much, why not get on at a national park. The rest…was history."

When he'd finished talking, Alex didn't say anything. Instead, she stared out the window at the passing scenery, giving him glimpses of her beautiful profile. He had a feeling she was trying to hide from him, but there was no place to go.

"Alex?" he prodded.

"What happened to you and your brother?" She was still turned away from him.

"Jack discovered Helen's promiscuity for himself and figured out she was the reason I left home. Once we'd talked, he divorced her. Today he's married to a wonderful woman and has four children. In the end we both got what we wanted."

Alex was too quiet. "Why are you telling me all this?"

His hands tightened on the steering wheel. "To help

you understand that my rejection of you over the years wasn't based on anything to do with you personally. The fact is, Helen was an exceptionally beautiful girl. So were you. She also came from a rich, prominent family like yours. When you came to the park, I made the mistake of drawing comparisons from the moment we met. It wasn't fair or logical. It was simply a gut reaction on my part."

"Six years is a long time to be mistaken about someone."

"I had a lot of help. Between your father, who let me know he expected me to protect you, and the Chief, who told me I could look, but not touch, I kept you at arm's length."

"Until I pulled a Helen on you," she muttered. "You must have been totally repulsed."

"Hardly. You remember what happened as well as I do. If you were listening the other night, I didn't kiss Helen back." He reached for her hand and clasped it. "You're not the person I thought you were."

"I still don't know what you're driving at. You fell in love with Leeann and married her. None of this is relevant." She moved her hand away.

"Except that she died, and my world changed again. You're here again and the old rules no longer apply. I want to get to know the real you and see where it leads."

Her head was lowered. "My world has changed, too, Cal. We're both different people now. The other day you asked if we could be friends. I think that's the best way for us to get along. I'll only be here until the end of July, maybe not even that long. It depends on the boys."

He took a deep breath. "What do you mean?"

"The tribal council was concerned the boys might get too homesick if they're gone so long. Depending on the feedback from them, Halian will ask for a vote at the end of June to see whether they should return home or stay through the end of July."

That was only two weeks away...

"Does Vance know about this?" Cal knew for a fact Jeff didn't, or his friend would have told him.

"Yes, but he was willing to risk it. In case we do go home early, the money from the Trent fund will still be in place to pay for replacement volunteers. The LTSY has lots of kids who'd be willing to come, so the park won't suffer any loss."

If Cal had been upset earlier over a possible relationship between her and Telford, it was nothing compared to the possibility that she might be gone by the end of the month.

He felt like a bottle in a lab filled with expensive chemicals. Except for one dangerous moment when he'd felt her mouth moving beneath his, he'd kept that bottle tightly corked because opening it would set off a chain reaction that would alter his universe. But her news had brought him to the point where he had to pop the cork or he was going to explode anyway.

"Cal?" Her voice brought him back from the edge. "Unless the boys are somewhere else, we just passed the turnoff for the Meadows."

"You're right, but there's a tourist in a red car up ahead who's been doing fifty in a thirty-five mile an hour zone for the last few minutes. Eight bears were killed in this area last year because of speeders. Two were hit and died since the opening of the Tioga road this year."

Cal turned on the siren and went after him.

AT ANY OTHER TIME SINCE Alex had known him, Cal's suggestion that they start a relationship would have been the fulfillment of a dream, but for some reason she felt numb inside. Despite everything he'd explained, Cal had married Leeann. He'd moved on. Alex didn't want to simply be a substitute.

While she sat there in a daze, Cal maneuvered through the traffic to pull the motorist over. He reached for his hat lying on the back floor and got out of the car. Sergei made whimpering sounds. No doubt he wanted to get out, too.

"He'll be right back," she said as she watched Cal approach the other vehicle. In full gear he was gorgeous, but he could also be intimidating, forbidding even.

She shivered and rested her head against the window, glad she wasn't the one receiving the ticket from him. It wouldn't stop there. Those intelligent eyes would turn a fierce blue while he gave the driver a much-needed verbal warning.

"Alex?" He called to her while she was deep in thought. "Are you all right?" He'd gotten back in the car and was staring at her in concern.

"I'm fine. I was just relaxing for a minute."

He let it go, but she could feel his tension. While traffic was still stopped, he made a U-turn and they headed back to the road leading to the north area.

Another minute and they were making their way to the campground filled with tourists ready to hike the

Glen Aulin trail. After he parked the car, she got out and looked around while Cal opened the door for Sergei and put him on leash.

He caught up to her. "Their work area is up in that meadow to the right beyond the trees. Shall we go?"

Cal led her through the underbrush away from everyone else. Once they got beyond the pines, the view opened on a hillside spattered with wildflowers. No sight in the high Sierras could match this for breathtaking beauty. Sergei must have thought so, too. You'd never know he'd hurt his paw the way he ambled up the incline alongside his master.

Here and there she spotted half a dozen volunteers in straw hats and gloves working six different grids. She watched as they painstakingly pulled out the flowering weeds. The thistles' unmistakable yellow heads were filled with seeds that needed to be destroyed. Once the plants were free of the soil, they were stuffed into doubled plastic bags. Alex counted at least seventy that had to be carted down to the road and taken away in trucks.

Cal waved to the supervisor, but kept on moving. Alex couldn't see the boys. She stopped at one point to look around. "Where do you suppose they are?"

"Their shift is over. They probably went to the river to cool off after work. We'll go see. In this heat Sergei could use a drink."

It was hot all right. As Alex quickened her pace to keep up with them, the dog started barking and pulled on the leash. Suddenly Mika and Lusio, still wearing their hats, their gloves tucked in their back pockets, came walking out of an upper pine belt that followed the lines of an ancient moraine. She expected to be greeted with smiles, but their expressions had closed up. Those dark solemn eyes meant something was wrong.

As soon as they approached, Sergei was all over them, sniffing and barking much more excitedly than usual.

Cal pulled him back. "What is it, buddy?"

Mika looked at Cal. "Come and see what we found a few minutes ago."

Alex looked at his companion. "Lusio?"

The other teen shook his dark head. "It's not good."

The boys were not given to overdramatize a situation, so Alex could tell that whatever they'd seen was not good. She needed to prepare herself.

The dog strained to break the leash as they made their way into the deepest part of the trees. Sergei suddenly let out a bone-chilling wail only an animal could make. That's when Alex saw the bodies of three bears, all cut open. The breath left her lungs.

"Look, Alex." Mika lifted one of the limbs. "Every paw has been cut off."

Lusio nodded. "The hunter took all their teeth."

Alex gasped. The sight was something out of a horror story. "I don't believe it." Her voice shook in rage.

A grim Cal was already down on his haunches examining the remains. She could sense his fury and everyone else's. In a minute he pulled out his phone to make his report while Sergio sniffed around.

After Cal hung up, his mournful gaze met to hers. "Chase is calling in the U.S. investigator for the National Park Service. He'll be bringing a couple of special agents from the Pacific West Region and several wardens from the California Fish and Game."

"What will they do?" Lusio asked.

"Once they find out who was involved in this massacre, they'll file multiple federal charges under the Lacey Act. That means the guys will go to prison."

Mika nodded. "That's good."

Alex stared at Cal. "Who would do such a thing? Why?"

"It's big business. This kind of carnage will have brought at least thirty thousand dollars to the twisted monsters who did the butchering."

"For what?"

"In certain markets bear paws go for a thousand dollars apiece. They're used to make soup, which is considered a delicacy. Some believe it's a curative for respiratory and gastrointestinal ailments. The teeth and claws are used to make ashtrays and jewelry."

Alex felt sick just thinking about it. "The cruelty is beyond my comprehension. How do they subdue the bears?"

Cal's jaw hardened. "First they lure them with food, then subdue them with an ultrahot bear spray and tranquilize them."

"They steal the tranquilizers?" Lusio questioned.

"That's right, Lusio. Whoever does this has no conscience. It's because there's a worldwide demand for authentic bear parts to be used in traditional Chinese medicine. These products are popular in Asian countries and communities. More and more we're finding bear carcasses discarded in forests like this in the U.S. because the Asian black bear population has declined. Our bears here are the new targets."

Alex hugged her arms to her waist, devastated by

the slaughter. The boys' Zuni heritage considered the animals sacred. She could only imagine how they were feeling. "But why were they cut open, too?"

"Pacific Rim nations use the bile of a black bear's gall bladder as a cure-all. The coveted acid is used for cancer and other treatments. It's dried, ground up and sold by the gram. The street value is higher than cocaine. Some galls are soaked in alcohol such as vodka and then consumed. One gall bladder can bring upwards of five thousand dollars."

"This was a recent kill," Lusio said. "Maybe night before last."

Cal nodded. "Then they sneaked away in the dark. Since the gall bladder is only as big as a person's thumb, it can be put in a jar in a backpack along with the other parts and no one is the wiser."

"The evil person could be hiking around Yosemite right now, looking for his next strike."

Mika's comment sent an icy chill across Alex's skin. She turned her head away, trying to hold back her revulsion.

"Alex? If you're up to it, I'd like you to drive the boys home."

She swung back. "I'm fine."

"Good. I'm going to be here for some time and don't want them to miss Ranger Farr's talk tonight. He gives a fascinating program about the water cycle in the park. Experts from around the world come to study our snow."

Alex realized Cal's suggestion was a veiled command. She needed to pull herself together. "I guess you want to keep Sergei with you."

His troubled gaze flicked over her. "This is part of his training and will make him even more valuable in the field."

Cal walked them to the edge of the trees and patted both boys on the shoulder. "Thank you for being so observant. All these people were around today, but you two were the ones who made the discovery. You have keen instincts I admire very much. There'll be a reward for this."

Her throat swelled with emotion because she knew his words had pleased them.

"Do me another favor?" All their eyes were still fastened on Cal. "Don't tell a soul what you've seen here. Not even Lonan. We need to behave as if nothing happened so the culprits won't pick up on it. Because this crime was found so fast, it's possible we'll catch this person or persons before long." The boys nodded.

He reached in his pocket and handed Alex the keys. "I'm going to ask another favor." His piercing blue eyes held hers. "Drive straight to my house. When you get there, call me and I'll phone Cindy. She'll give you a ride back to Sugar Pines."

She studied him. "When will you come home?"

"I'm not sure. One of the other rangers will bring me."

Alex got a sinking feeling in the pit of her stomach. An emergency of this magnitude superseded anything else on his agenda. "These people must be very dangerous."

The way he looked at her raised the hairs on the back of her neck. "Especially if they think you or the boys know anything. Be careful, trust no one, and above all, drive safely."

Alex had a feeling he knew a lot more than he was telling her. "I was going to say the same thing to you."

"It's nice to know I have a friend who cares," he said in a voice so deep it rumbled through her.

She didn't want to be his friend.

I wanted you! All of you. Your body, your soul. But Leeann was the one you wanted and I can't accept that.

Alex leaned over to scratch Sergei behind the ears. "Be a good boy. Mind Cal."

The dog tried to follow her, but the leash would only let him go so far. She heard his bark as if he were trying to call her back. She sensed Cal was still watching them, but kept walking with the boys.

Once they reached the car and headed for the Valley she said, "You guys were real heroes today. You know that?"

"We didn't do anything," Mika muttered.

"What if you hadn't gone exploring after work? Those bear remains might not have been found for a long time. At least this way there's a fighting chance Cal will be able to apprehend whoever did that crime much sooner."

She heard them talking quietly in the back. Suddenly Mika said her name in a way that told her something important was on his mind.

"What is it?"

"Lusio and I just remembered something about when we were up at Tenaya Lake."

"Go on."

"You know Steve?"

"After how badly he made you feel, I'm not likely to forget him."

"When he opened his backpack to get out his insect repellent, he must have opened the wrong compartment because we saw bear spray. He zipped it up again real fast."

She tensed.

"We thought only the chaperones were supposed to carry it."

So did Alex. "Maybe Mr. Thorn told his kids to bring some along."

"Then Steve must have brought it for the others—we counted at least six cans," Lusio informed her. "It didn't seem important at the time, but when we found those bears today and Cal told us how bear spray is used to subdue them, it got us thinking."

"Now you've got me thinking. I'm glad you told me. I'll pass the information on to Cal."

Two hours later she said goodbye to the boys at Curry Village. They wanted to get tacos first, then walk back to Sugar Pines. Alex told them to have fun, knowing they wouldn't mention anything about the bears.

After she reached Cal's house and put his car away, she phoned him to let him know she was back.

"I'm glad you got there safely. Cindy will be by for you in a few minutes. Just leave the car keys on the counter in the kitchen and lock the front door as you leave. Alex—" he sounded intense "—I'd like to talk to you longer, but we're in the middle of this investigation. Got to run."

He hung up before she could tell him about her

conversation with the boys. While she waited outside for her ride, she decided to let Vance know what she'd learned. Unfortunately he wasn't answering, so she left a voice message for him to call her back ASAP.

Before long Cindy pulled in the drive and Alex climbed in her truck. After they'd backed out and started down the street, the pretty ranger cocked her head. Her hazel eyes seemed to be asking a question. "What's going on with you and Ranger Hollis? For you to be driving his car today is a first."

Alex had to be careful how she answered. Cal wanted the news about the bears kept secret. "He got detained on business and couldn't bring the boys back from their work project. It made sense for me to drive them. He said he'd get a ride later with one of the other rangers."

"I don't mean just today."

"Oh."

"As long as I've worked here, there's always been something between you two." Alex's heartbeat sped up. *Always?* "I've never been able to figure it out."

Alex decided to joke about it. "There's nothing to figure out. I usually tagged along with my father when he came to the park. I'm not proud to admit I was a big pain, but Cal and I have achieved a working pax now."

A shadow fell across her face. "You know what happened to his wife?"

She took a quick breath. "Yes. I can't imagine anything more ghastly."

"It was awful."

"Were you good friends with her?"

"As much as we could be without knowing each other

very long." Cindy seemed to hesitate. "Please don't take this wrong, but Leeann used to worry about you."

That was news. "In what way?"

"She'd heard about you and thought maybe you were the reason Cal was so slow to commit to her."

Alex laughed to hide her pain. "Me? The senator's obnoxious daughter? If he was slow, it had nothing to do with me. He asked *her* to marry him."

"That's true."

Alex was still reeling from the revelation when they pulled into Sugar Pines. Before she opened the door, she turned to Cindy. "How would you like to go to lunch at the Yosemite Lodge next week? My treat. I'd like to pay you back for driving me home."

"I'd love it. We could swim first."

"Great."

"What day would be best?"

"How about Wednesday? That's my day off."

"Perfect. I'll call you for a definite time. Thanks for the ride."

She hurried inside the ski lodge, glad to see Lusio and Mika had made it back from town. Sheila, the director, was crossing through the lounge and told her the ranger presentation would be starting soon.

"Has Lonan's fiancée arrived?"

"Yes. They're outside at the amphitheater with some of the boys waiting for the program to begin."

Alex had just enough time to grab a bite to eat from the kitchen before she went out to join them. Happy as she was that Mankanita had come, she couldn't get her mind off the men who'd mutilated those bears. If they thought Cal was getting too close, they might try to harm him.

Along with that fear, his revelations about why he'd rejected Alex for so long were starting to sink in. He wouldn't lie to her, would he?

And then she had Cindy's remark about Leeann to think about. She needed to be alone, but that wasn't possible right now. Everyone was waiting for her. It was going to be hard to go out there and pretend all was well, but she had no choice. The boys were depending on her.

Chapter Nine

Before Cal reported to the Chief's office Saturday morning for an emergency meeting, he and Sergei made a detour to Ranger Sim's office. He hoped the head of security had managed to dig up some background information on a couple of unsolved bear mutilation crimes that could help him with this latest investigation.

When he entered his office, he found Jeff hunched over Sim's desk supplying input. Both heads came up before his friend hurried forward. He gave Sergei a brief rubdown, then looked at Cal. "That was some find those boys came across yesterday."

"It was ugly, Jeff."

"How did you get here so fast?" Sims called out.

"Vance sent a helicopter to fly me and the investigators back early this morning for Bishop. We worked half the night before crashing at the Rim Rock motel. I had to cancel my meeting with the forest service heads."

"This matter has taken precedence over everything. I'm glad you're here. We'd better get in there, too. The Superintendent's antsy this morning."

Cal had news for him. Bill Telford was always like that.

The three men headed out the door and down the hall. Beth stood outside Vance's office redirecting traffic because the meeting place had been changed. Coffee and doughnuts now awaited them in the conference room.

"I haven't seen this many rangers assembled in ages," Jeff whispered as they made their way around the table to find a seat. Sergei lay down by Cal.

"Let's hope it produces results." The mutilation deaths of three bears had brought in the big brass.

Bill Telford spoke first, acknowledging everyone's presence. "The element of secrecy is crucial right now, gentlemen. What's important is that we carry on this investigation without the press getting hold of any information yet. It could tip off the criminals. With that said, we'll hear first from Nate Daniels, the special investigator."

The man who'd gone over the crime scene with Cal stood up. "Gentlemen? Ranger Jarvis called in our department the minute Ranger Hollis alerted him to the find. In our opinion this is the most egregious case of illegal bear hunting and killing we've uncovered here in Yosemite in years.

"As Ranger Hollis has stated, the wildlife in the park is as important as Half Dome or Yosemite Falls. Our department is taking this crime very seriously and will continue to aggressively investigate and prosecute anybody found to be partaking in this activity. It's a very serious offense and we want to send a clear message that it will not be tolerated. Chief Rossiter has more to say on that."

It was a rare sight to see Vance's countenance so dark. He looked around the table. "We've got a real menace on our hands. It's no news to any of you that poaching is a problem in every national park. We've already got our hands full with the deaths of too many mule deers.

"At my last conference with other chiefs, it became clear there's seemingly nothing poachers won't take, be it snakes from Mojave National Preserve, fossils from Badlands National Park in South Dakota, American ginseng from Shenandoah National Park in Virginia or frontier-era pistols from Fort Davis National Historic Site in Texas."

Cal was aware of most of the poaching Vance spoke of, but not the theft of pistols.

"To quote the chief at Yellowstone, 'There are no resources out there, besides air, that someone isn't taking unlawfully.' We know a huge segment of the population is commercially removing park resources. Just last week Ranger Hollis discovered increased theft of downed redwood trees within our park boundaries. This affects the future survival of our park, since new trees take root in the fallen ones and fertilize the next generation.

"Our forests were set aside for the enjoyment of all people, yet less than five percent of all the old-growth redwoods in the world remain. For people to steal them is a major crime. They work at night when few people are around to hear their chain saws. The forest's heavy growth does a remarkable job muffling the sound. The thieves work over the course of several nights, coming and going at random times to evade detection."

It was impossible to miss the anger in the chief's voice. "I'm convinced this is what these ruthless bear hunters are doing under our very noses. They do it noiselessly, and their ability to hide what they take without anyone being aware makes them especially deadly. Therefore I'm asking you to inform all the people working under you to be more alert than ever before. Anything they see that sends up a red flag, no matter how unimportant it seems, we'll investigate. Ranger Sims will spell out your job in more detail."

Ranger Sims took over. "As head of Homeland Security and Terror watch, you all know it's my job along with Ranger Jarvis to vet not only the entire population of employees within the park, but to keep track of every visitor coming and going. Because of the gravity of this case, I've asked for Ranger Thompson's help because he oversees the volunteer program, which brings in another segment of the population for seasonal work. We're not leaving a stone unturned to catch these criminals."

All around the table, the rangers nodded or voiced their agreement.

"As a result we're going to be doing more thorough checks of people's belongings and vehicles along with surprise random checks," Sims continued. "Bikers, hikers, volunteers, everyone working the concessions, road and maintenance people—no one will be exempt. Ranger Hollis is going to tell you what you'll be looking for."

Cal went over the list with them. When he finished, the meeting broke up. Vance asked him and Jeff to stay. After the treats were consumed, the room cleared except for Chase. The Chief locked the door, then sat back down at the table.

"We have a glimmer of a possible lead in this case," he announced, "but I didn't want it going beyond the four of us yet. It came from Alex."

It wouldn't have surprised Cal if everyone felt the body-rocking thump of his heart. "How? When?"

"She phoned me yesterday and I called her back later last evening. It seems that on her drive back to Sugar Pines, the boys told her they'd seen cans of bear spray in the backpack of one of the volunteers in Ralph Thorn's group. They noticed it when he opened his pack to get out some insect repellent at Tenaya Lake."

"What?"

In the next breath Vance told them what had happened to Alex and her group on that outing.

Cal's hands formed fists. "I wonder what else was in that backpack. What's the teen's name?"

"Steve Minor."

The revelation drove Cal out of his chair, startling the dog. "I don't understand. Why didn't she tell me Thorn had left her alone so long to go off with Steve?"

Vance stared up at him. "It's because she was operating in secret for me."

For the first time since Cal had known Vance, he was confused. "Am I missing something?"

"It's my fault you're full of questions," he admitted. "When I told Alex she was hired as a volunteer for the summer, I gave her the extra job of being my personal liaison."

Cal was stunned. That was tantamount to Vance making her an honorary ranger.

"She was to report to me and no one else. I had no idea she'd stumble across something this serious so soon."

Cal stared at him. On an intellectual level he understood Vance's reasons for wanting another pair of eyes, but emotionally he feared for her safety.

"If this lead turns out to help us catch this monster, then Alex's help is paying dividends in a number of ways. At every campground she's visited so far, she's uncovered violation after violation. Already she's sent in a ton of license plate numbers where food has been left on seats in vehicles."

That was why the rangers had been giving out a slew of tickets lately? Cal had never seen so many in such a short time.

"So far she's worth her weight in gold," Vance said with quiet satisfaction.

Adrenaline charged Cal's nervous system. Maybe that was true, but it potentially put her life at risk. His thoughts shot ahead. "She's with Thorn and his group today."

"I know. I asked her to keep her eyes open, Cal. Alex and the boys know what's at stake. When she reports back to me, we'll find out what she's learned—if anything. What have you discovered on your end, Jeff?"

"Steve Minor was one of the volunteers last year. He's also in the same school district in Torrance where Ralph Thorn is the psychologist."

Vance eyed the three of them. "It's a possible tie-in. If Thorn is one of the criminals, he might have some kind of hold on Steve and is using him."

Jeff held out several papers. "Here are their applications for this year and last, both with picture ID."

Chase took them from Jeff. "I'll go back to my office right now and run them through the national data base for possible aliases or warrants for their arrest that weren't added at the time."

"Something tells me we're working with more than

two people," Cal muttered. "Come on, Jeff. Let's go through the volunteer applications to see if there's anything we've missed."

"Cal?" Vance had gotten to his feet. He patted the dog, eyeing both of them. "I'm glad you and Jeff know about Alex. Keep an eye on her as a personal favor to me. And watch your back," he added.

He blinked. "What do you mean?"

"Alex has the feeling Thorn doesn't like you for some reason."

Cal knew another volunteer who didn't like him, either. Brock Giolas.

Interesting.

He and Jeff nodded before walking back to his office. Once they were alone, Jeff gave Cal one of those inscrutable looks.

"What?" Cal blurted with impatience. Vance's revelation about Alex had shaken him.

"The way you react every time Alex's name is brought up—it makes me think you're in love with her. How about telling me what's going on? They say confession's good for the soul. I'm no priest, but I'm willing to listen as long as it's the whole truth."

Cal shot his dark-haired friend a penetrating glance. "Have you got all day?"

ALEX'S GROUP REACHED the Hetch Hetchy Valley campground before Ralph's. They all stopped to drink the water they'd brought and feast their eyes on the view. Mankanita walked over to Alex.

"Thank you for making it possible for me to come."

"Lonan has missed you."

Mankanita got a sweet look on her face. "I've missed him, too. I can see why you love it here so much. Lonan told me it was beautiful. He was right." The Valley resembled the Yosemite Valley and was an awe-inspiring sight. Mankanita's response was all Alex could have hoped for.

As she turned around to see how everyone was doing, she let out a little gasp because Cal had unexpectedly appeared with Chief Sam Dick and his wife. The older couple wore ceremonial dress.

Cal's blue gaze zeroed in on Alex. She felt a quickening in her body as they stared at each other. He hadn't brought Sergei. Soon Ralph and his group arrived. She saw the way his eyes narrowed when he caught sight of Cal, who told all the kids to form a semicircle and sit down to hear the old chief speak.

Alex sat at one end of her group, Lonan and Mankanita at the other. Ralph and his kids formed the second and third tiers. Chief Sam stood a little way off, the backdrop of the valley providing an impressive natural surrounding. His wife sat next to him.

When everyone was settled, Cal stepped forward. He looked magnificent in his uniform, Alex thought. The late-afternoon sun gilded his dark blond hair. Out of respect for the chief, he'd removed his hat. Both men came from different times and cultures. Both were noble and strong. A surge of emotions without words filled her.

"You teens have the unprecedented honor of gathering at the feet of one of the great Paiute Chiefs of Yosemite. He's going to tell you a legend about his land and his people."

The next thing Alex knew, Cal came to sit next to her so their legs touched. At the first contact, fire as real as a burning torch scorched across her skin. The moment was surreal.

The chief looked out over them with visionary eyes. "I used to hunt acorns here. My people called this place Ahwahnee. It means 'large mouth,' like the bear's. The white man calls it Yosemite. In our language it means, 'those who kill.' Many generations ago before the Creator completed the fashioning of the cliffs in the Valley of the Ahwahnee, a Paiute couple lived at Mono Lake. They learned of the beautiful and fertile Valley of Ahwahnee and decided to come here to dwell.

"They began their journey. He carried deer skins. She held a baby in her arms and carried a wono basket on her back. When they reached Mirror Lake, they began to quarrel. She wanted to go back to Mono Lake, but he refused. No oaks or other trees grew there. He would not listen to her when she said she would plant seeds."

While he was speaking, Alex felt Cal's hand cover hers beneath the hat he'd put down. He squeezed it gently, but didn't let go.

"In despair, the girl began to cry and ran back toward the Paiute homeland of Mono Lake. Her husband grew angry and ran after her. To escape she threw the wono basket at him and it became Basket Dome. She continued running and threw the baby cradle at her husband. That is what we call Royal Arches."

Alex looked at the boys beside her. They were spellbound by the chief's story.

"Because they had brought anger into Yosemite, the Creator became upset at the couple and turned them into stone. He became North Dome and she became Half Dome. The Mono Lake Paiute girl regretted the quarrel. Half Dome began to cry and formed Mirror Lake.

"Today you can still see the marks of the tears on her face looking toward Mono Lake. If you look carefully at Half Dome, you can see it is fashioned after the way of the Paiute. The first white explorers called her South Dome. Later she was called Half Dome. But in Paiute she is known as T'ssiyakka, girl who cries. Many white men changed the names. Do you not find it so?" He was addressing Lonan.

"Yes. My people came to the middle place Halona and were called A'shiwi, meaning 'the flesh.' The Spaniards called us Zuni. It had no meaning for us."

The chief nodded. "Such is the way." He looked around. "Do any of you have questions?"

One by one the kids raised their hands and a marvelous dialogue took place. Cal kept Alex's hand enveloped in his the entire time, occasionally smoothing his thumb over the pulse at her wrist. After a half hour he leaned close to her. "The chief would never admit he's tired, but I know he is, so I'm going to end things. I'll walk you back to the lodge."

He let her go and stood up, taking his hat and his warmth with him. "We want to thank the chief and his wife for making this trip unforgettable for us. The best way we can do that is to take care of the land and the animals while we're here. Come and shake hands with Chief Sam Dick and his wife before they leave in their car."

All the way down the mountain Alex had to pinch herself that Cal was walking at her side, let alone that she'd been granted the privilege of being part of this moving experience. The exchange of cultures had succeeded in openings up Ralph's volunteers to Alex's group. They asked more questions of Alex's boys and chatted with Lonan and Mankanita all the way to the lodge tucked away in the forest.

Once they arrived, everyone split up to have fun in the recreation center or eat a meal on the deck. Cal followed her to an empty table and pulled out a chair for her. The way he was treating her, Ralph would have every reason to believe the two of them were a couple.

Cal smiled as he sat down opposite her. "We could join Lonan, but I think he'd rather be alone with his fiancée."

She nodded. The setting was terribly romantic. "Why didn't you bring Sergei?"

"He got a big workout yesterday. Today I decided to let him rest his paw."

"That's probably a good idea."

Once the waitress came to take their orders, Cal put the menu down and glanced at Alex. "I don't know about you, but this was a red-letter day for me."

"You already know how I feel about it. I wonder how old the chief is. One day he won't be here and a whole era will be gone we can't ever get back."

His expression sobered. He started to say something, but his phone rang. "Excuse me, Alex, but I'm still on duty."

She watched him leave the table and walk over to the edge of the deck where he could talk privately. With the bear mutilations on his mind, he was probably waiting to hear about any leads in the case. So was she.

By the time he returned, their dinner had arrived. "I hate to eat and run, but that was the special agent working on the bear case. I've got to get back to headquarters stat." He wolfed down his burger and put a couple of bills on the table. His eyes darted to hers. "Enjoy the rest of your evening. I'll see you sometime tomorrow after you're back. Drive safely."

She wished the same for him, but he'd moved too fast for her to say so. Before she had time to examine all her chaotic feelings, Mika and Lusio joined her at the table.

"We've got something to tell you."

AT TWO O'CLOCK THE NEXT DAY she met with Chief Rossiter and repeated what the boys had said. She'd let her kids off in the Yosemite Lodge parking lot so they could eat and enjoy the rest of their day off. Lonan had gone with Mankanita, who had to drive to Merced for the flight back to Albuquerque.

Alex planned to grab a meal at Curry Village, but first she hurried over to headquarters where Vance was waiting for her.

"During our hike to and from the Hetch Hetchy yesterday," she said as soon as she was seated, "our groups separated for a while so I had no way of knowing about Steve's or Ralph's activities the whole time. After we reached the Evergreen Lodge, Mika and Lusio headed for the restroom, but they hid themselves when they saw Ralph come out with Brock Giolas."

Alex hesitated. She hadn't been sure at first whether she should report this to the chief or not, then decided it could be significant.

"I think the meeting of those two men was too much of a coincidence. You see, during orientation Brock asked me to eat lunch with him. A week later he wanted me to go hiking. Both times I turned him down. When I think about it, both times happened to be when Cal was around. Brock asked me if Cal and I were an item. I told him no."

Vance's eyes flickered as she spoke.

"From the beginning Brock knew I was a chaperone along with Ralph and the others. If he's being friendly with Ralph to find out if I lied to him about Cal—and asked Ralph to spy on me—that's one thing."

"But if he and Ralph have known each other before—" the Chief anticipated her thoughts "—then their connection might have to do with the bear mutilations." He smiled slightly. "You know, it could be a case of both of them simply being attracted to you, which would be no surprise to anyone."

Her cheeks went warm. "Brock maybe, not Ralph."

He shook his head. "I disagree, but be extra careful, Alex. You may be on to something. As for the boys—"

"Don't worry. I had a talk with them. They know better than to do anything that will draw attention."

"Good. As I've told you before, phone me day or night if there's anything you're concerned about."

"I promise."

When she left headquarters, a truck slowed down in front of her. Sergei was in the bed, looking over the side at her. He barked a greeting. Cal sat behind the wheel looking altogether too attractive.

He opened the passenger door, and Alex saw that handsome, hard-boned face badly needed a shave. Beneath the rim of his hat, his heavily lashed eyes, dark as cobalt, traveled over her. She wondered how long it had been since he'd slept.

"I take it you've been inside to see the Chief."

"Yes. Now I'm going back to camp."

"Come home with me instead. After I shower, I'll make us some sandwiches."

At this point Alex had so little willpower where he was concerned, it terrified her. She wanted to take him up on his offer, but she'd had a whole night to think about what it meant. If all he wanted was a fling until she flew home to New Mexico, she didn't dare get any closer to him. "Thanks, but I need to get back to camp. My minibus is right over there."

"Your boys can phone you if they need anything. I'll take you back to your bus later. I'm off duty until tomorrow."

Hardening herself she said, "With those eyelids drooping from no sleep, I'm surprised you haven't already passed out in your truck. You don't need company."

"But *you* need protecting," he replied in a no-nonsense tone.

"What do you mean?"

"Vance told me about your liaison job with him. After what's been happening around here, he had to confide in me."

Her spirits took a downward spiral. For the second time since she'd arrived at the park, Cal had said something unexpected, crushing the tendril of hope that had sprung forth since their last talk. She struggled to maintain her composure. "I see."

"You and the boys have been caught in the middle of

something big. Now that I've been apprised of all the facts, I can't let you go back to the ski lodge until tonight, when Lonan will be there after seeing Mankanita off. Jeff's talking to him now so he understands what's at stake here."

Under the circumstances, Alex had little choice but to climb in the cab and shut the door. This was Ranger Hollis, not Cal, giving her an order, and he had the full backing of federal legal authority his office granted him.

They didn't speak the rest of the way to his house. By the time he'd pulled into the garage, the tension had become unbearable. She got out as fast as she could, thankful the dog was there to provide needed relief.

"Would you like me to take Sergei for a short walk while you freshen up?"

Cal fastened the leash before handing it to her. His fingers brushed hers, sending rivulets of fire through her body. "Be back in five minutes. I'll leave the garage door open for you."

"Did you hear that, Sergei? Let's go!"

HE WATCHED THE TWO of them walk away. She was upset. The set of her jaw, the spots of color in her cheeks gave her away. When she returned, he wouldn't rest until they talked.

In a few swift strides he reached the bathroom. One look in the mirror filled him with disgust. A shower and shave did a little to clean him up, but he couldn't wash away the fatigue. He'd been up on a grueling all-nighter with the Feds heading the investigation and needed a block of undisturbed sleep.

After brushing his teeth, he threw on his toweling robe and walked down the hall to his bedroom to get dressed. Once he'd slipped on jeans and a polo shirt, he passed the spare bedroom and saw Alex down on the carpet on her stomach, looking at the painting that rested against the wall.

In her right hand she still held one of Sergei's toys, evidence she'd been playing tug-of-war with him. He lay on his front paws watching her.

Once before he'd seen her on the floor. She'd been in the kitchen and he'd wanted to join her. This time he didn't hesitate and lay down next to her. She let out a little cry of surprise. He captured the hand that held the toy, preventing her from getting up.

"I've always wanted to know if you picked out this painting, Alex." At the sound of his voice, Sergei inched his way closer to them.

"No. This is Dad through and through," she said in a husky tone. "He loves history. If I'd had my way, I would have given you a painting of Sunset Butte, my favorite spot on the ranch. It's all orange and purple in the dying sun."

Beneath his fingers he could feel her trembling, and he could no longer hold back. Leaning over, he kissed the nape of her neck. She was so sweet. So delectable. Yet the minute he felt her warmth and tasted her fragrant skin, it wasn't enough. He found himself rolling her on her back to kiss the lips that had been haunting him for what seemed like forever.

"You're so beautiful. You always were. I never told you before, but I'm telling you now. Do you have any idea how wonderful you are? How much I want to make love to you?" He leaned down to cover her mouth with his own.

But she didn't open up to him like she'd done at the lookout tower. Instead she turned her head to the side. "Once upon a time I threw myself at you, dying to hear those words, Cal. But that time has passed." She rolled away from him and stood up, ready to bolt from his house. Sergei imitated her, wanting to play some more.

Cal got to his feet. He was nearest the door. "What's wrong?"

Her features were drawn tight. "I'd like to trust you, but I can't."

"Why?"

"For as long as we've known each other, I've been a project to you one way or the other. Now that you know Vance has hired me to be his liaison, you feel an extra responsibility. You're so used to looking after me, I don't think you know what you're feeling. I'm not blaming you for it, but it's very unsettling for me. Would you please drive me back to my bus?"

Cal couldn't tell her no, but he was hurting. "If that's what you want."

She rubbed Sergei's head before looking over at Cal. Her smile didn't reach her eyes. "Friends?"

"You're more than a friend to me, Alex."

"I heard a country-and-western song the other day called 'I Think I'll Pass.' You could have supplied the inspiration for the lyrics. The end went something like, 'I'm more than a friend, less than a wife—good for the moment, just not his whole life—I think I'll pass.' Have you ever noticed that country-and-western composers write true to life?"

While he stood there feeling gutted, she stepped past him. "I'll wait for you in the truck."

Sergei followed her out. Cal knew when she'd gone into the garage because his dog came back with his head down, making whining noises. He went into to his bedroom to grab the keys off his dresser. "You don't know the half of it, buddy. Not the half."

"THANKS FOR THE RIDE, CAL." They'd driven in silence to the parking lot near the Yosemite Lodge. Alex patted Sergei's head, glad the place was crowded with tourists. Cal had to drive on once she got down from the cab because other cars were waiting. She could hear the truck engine as she climbed inside her minibus. For a minute she rested her forehead against the steering wheel, waiting for that feeling of weakness to pass.

"Hi, Alex! Can we get a ride to Roberta's house with you?"

She turned her head to discover Nicky and Roberta standing outside the door. "Hey, you two! Sure you can. Climb on in."

"Thanks. It's too hot out." They took seats in front beside her and buckled up.

Alex was in so much turmoil she'd hardly noticed the heat, but they were right. This afternoon was a scorcher. She closed the doors and they took off. "What have you guys been up to?"

"Dad took us swimming," Roberta informed her.

"But it's too hot to do anything else outside," Nicky said, "so we're going to play at her house."

"That sounds fun. You'll have to tell me where to drive. I haven't been to your house before."

They directed her down a couple of streets.

"There's Mom!"

Alex pulled to a stop in front of the house. Annie Jarvis walked over to the curb. After what had just happened with Cal, Alex was in no state to talk to anyone, but she didn't want to be rude. Roberta's mother was an archaeologist. If she had time right now, Alex would be a fool not to take advantage of it.

Annie, a beautiful brunette, was dressed in shorts. She'd been watering some flowers in her garden. Alex turned off the motor and the three of them got out of the bus.

"That was nice of you to bring the kids home," Annie said. "I hope it wasn't too far out of your way."

"Heavens, no. I was just driving back to Sugar Pines to see how the boys are doing."

"Chase tells me they're really starting to fit in."

She nodded. "I know they love it here. Every day I see them opening up a little more to other people and possibilities. That's why I want them to meet you. Now that Chief Sam Dick has talked to them, they're much more curious about the petroglyphs around here."

"Roberta told me. I was going to call you next week."

"Is there a night you could come to the amphitheater and speak to the kids?"

"Sure. I'm free this coming Thursday."

"Then we'll do it."

"Do you want some mint lemonade?" Roberta called out. "Nicky and I are going to make some."

"I'd love it."

After the children ran into the house, Annie eyed her with interest. "I saw you in Cal Hollis's truck when the two of you drove by a little while ago. You can tell me to mind my own business if you want, but I know there's something's going on between the two of you. Since Chase and I had a long history, I recognize the signs."

A sigh escaped Alex's lips. "Except that Cal didn't have amnesia like your husband."

"Would it shock you to know that for a long time, I refused to accept what he told me? Ten years had gone by."

"I admit that would be hard to deal with."

"So hard I almost lost him because I had too much pride to give us a chance."

"Chase's story was different, Annie. When he recovered, he remembered that he loved you. The situation with me and Cal can't be compared. For one thing, he never loved me and he married Leeann."

Annie cocked her head. "Chase told me you started coming to the park with your father at least six years ago. Do you mean to tell me that in all that time, the interest was only on your part? Cal never once gave you the slightest hint that he had feelings for you?"

Alex sucked in her breath. She'd bottled so much inside. It was a relief to talk to someone, and Alex knew she could trust Annie. "He always looked at me like he was interested, but he never acted on it. Not until I did something that I'm still ashamed about." In a torrent of words, she told her what happened at the lookout tower.

"And it was after that he got married. Is that what you're saying?"

She nodded.

"Then why has he been hovering around you since you started your volunteer work?"

"Because Leeann is gone, and he assumes I'm still available for a brief fling."

"Did he tell you that's all he wants?"

"He admits to wanting me. He said I was more than a friend to him, but I didn't want to hear anything else and asked him to drive me to my bus."

Annie's brows lifted. "I didn't want to hear any more from Chase, either. But my parents cautioned me not to let my pride get in the way. I decided to take their advice and you know what happened. I've never been happier in my life. Not many people know yet, but we're expecting another baby. I had it confirmed when I went to San Francisco."

"Oh, how wonderful! Roberta must be overjoyed."

"Not to mention her parents." Annie smiled. "It's another miracle. Chase was told the injuries that caused his amnesia would make it virtually impossible for him to get a woman pregnant, but once again we've defied the odds."

With eyes brimming over, Alex gave her a congratulatory hug.

"Just remember something, Alex. Cal didn't have to take you to his house today in front of everyone. We both know what an extremely private man he is. So now that he's finally ready to talk, maybe you should listen. If nothing comes of it, then at least you will have done everything you could. That's when you'll start to heal."

"Come and get it!" Roberta called to them from the porch.

"We're coming, darling!"

"Thanks for the talk, Annie. I'll think about what you said."

They walked up the steps. "This lemonade is delicious with mint," Alex said after she'd taken a sip from the glass Roberta handed her.

"Thanks. My nana taught me to put some in."

"I just heard you're going to be getting a little brother or sister one of these days."

The twelve-year-old beamed.

"Have you picked out names yet?"

"If it's a girl we're going to call her Maggie."

"I love it. And if it's a boy?"

"They're going to call him Yosemite Sam," Nicky declared.

Both Annie and Alex laughed till they cried. It gave Alex a much-needed release from her tumultuous emotions. When she'd left Cal's house, she wouldn't have thought she could find anything funny.

Chapter Ten

After a fitful sleep, Cal awakened at two in the morning, knowing he'd never get any more rest. There wasn't anything he could do about Alex right now, but he could do some investigating on his own.

He fixed a breakfast of eggs and bacon, swallowed two cups of hot coffee and took off for Tenaya Lake with Sergei. If he got there before sunrise, he'd be able to hike to the area where Ralph Thorn had supposedly lost his cell phone. The outside chance he might uncover a piece of evidence while he looked around was worth the search.

So far none of the rangers had come across anything, but their workload was stretched. To do a thorough investigation took a lot of time. Since he couldn't be with Alex, it was the kind of work he would relish tonight.

By four-thirty, he and Sergei had reached the lodge-pole pines. The sky had started to get that pinkish pre-light color that made Tenaya Lake arguably one of the most gorgeous places in the park.

He walked it in a grid, covering section after section. Sergei stayed with him, sniffing everything imaginable. When Cal suddenly heard a howl, he thought it had to be a coyote watching them from close by, but it was his dog. Sergei yanked on the leash, trying to reach something he could smell.

"You've scented bears, huh, buddy? Let's go!" Cal ran up the mountain, trying to keep pace with Sergei, who was barking his head off. Another few feet and he came to a place in the forest where pine boughs covered part of the ground in unnatural fashion. His dog burrowed right into them.

Pulling out his flashlight, Cal shone it around. No sign of a bear. Then he hunkered down to remove one of the boughs. Beneath it were two large camouflage bags. "Well, what do we have here?" While the dog continued to bark, Cal undid the opening on the first one and discovered canisters of bear spray.

When he saw the contents of the second bag, he drew out his phone and called Chase. "Sorry to bother you this early in the morning, but Sergei just sniffed out something that's going to speed up the investigation."

"Where are you?"

Cal gave him the coordinates. "I don't want to touch anything in case fingerprints can be lifted, but there's bear spray, a dozen chisels, hacksaws, pliers—all the tools of the bear mutilation trade. Several of the hunting knives still have blood on them. This is obviously one of the drop-off places where they stash everything. It took several trips for them to pack in this stuff. Without my dog, I would never have found it."

"I'm on it, Cal. Fantastic work. Stay put. I'll be there with Nate's team of investigators shortly."

When he hung up, Cal hugged his dog. "Good job, Sergei. Good boy." He reached in his pocket and pulled out some doggie treats for him. "You're a keeper, you know that?" While he waited, he phoned Lonan, who now knew about the mutilated bears. Cal told him what he'd just found.

"I have to follow up on this now. Will you do me a favor and watch out for Mika and Lusio when they get back from the Meadows today? I haven't called Alex yet, but I'd like to take her back to the Hetch Hetchy with me so she can show me where Ralph went during the hike. We might not get back in time for her to eat dinner at the ski lodge with your group."

"No problem, Cal. I'll take care of everything."

"You're a good man, Lonan. I'll be in touch."

Before long a helicopter arrived bringing Vance, as well. Once the area had been thoroughly gone over, everyone rushed to tell Sergei he was a good dog and give him a vigorous rubdown, the kind he loved.

The Chief looked especially pleased. "We may not have caught the criminals yet, but we've got the weapons. You know what this means? Telford's going to find a way to fund more dogs for us."

That was outstanding news, but right now Cal's mind was on Alex. "Vance? If it's all right with you, I'm going to head over to the Hetch Hetchy with Alex so she can show me where she went with her group. Lonan will be in charge of the boys until she returns. Maybe there's another stash of tools hiding somewhere, or more bear carcasses. If so, Sergei will find them."

While they were hiking, Alex would have no choice but to hear him out. She *had* to listen to him. Their happiness depended on it.

"Go ahead, Cal, but be careful. With criminals this

brazen, there's no telling what they'll do if they feel cornered."

"I'm way ahead of you, Vance."

He hurried back to his truck. Once Sergei climbed in, he took off and phoned Alex. By now she ought to be up. She answered on the third ring. "Hello?"

"It's Cal."

There was a prolonged silence before she said, "Is something wrong?"

She had a habit of worrying. He doubted she'd ever break it. "No. I'm calling because I could use your help. This is official business. Just so you know, you don't have to do this. It's not an order."

Silence.

"Alex?" he prodded.

"I—I didn't behave well yesterday. I'm sorry."

His heart started to hammer. "No apology necessary. I'm the one who came on like gangbusters, as my grandfather used to say." She laughed. The sound was even more encouraging. "I'm taking Sergei to do some fieldwork at the Hetch Hetchy this morning. If you came with us, you could show me where your group hiked. I just want to take a look around."

"What about the boys?"

"I've already spoken to Lonan. He'll be in charge until we get back."

"I see. So you're planning to come by for me? I don't know if that's a good idea in case Ralph sees you."

"Alex—I'm not in the Valley. I'll meet you at the Evergreen Lodge. We'll eat before we head out. Bring your backpack and water."

"But Lonan has to drive the minibus today."

"Ask him to run you by headquarters now. Beth's there and will give you my house key. There's a duplicate car key in the left drawer in the kitchen so you can drive my Xterra. You've done it before. It's filled with gas."

"All right. I'll see you there. Where are you now?"

"I just left Tenaya Lake. I'll tell you all about it later."

He hung up before she could change her mind. En route to the other side of the park he phoned Jeff to fill him in. The news about the find was good, but it was a miracle Alex had agreed to meet him. He couldn't think beyond that.

AFTER LEAVING THE O'Shaughnessy Dam, the wildflowers on the hike to the base of Wapama Falls robbed Alex of words. The twelve-hundred-foot drop of water made a spectacular sight.

What an irony to be alone with Cal like this. Once it had been her dream. Now that she'd finally gotten her wish, it hit her as never before there was nothing worse than broken dreams.

But she'd decided to take Annie's advice. If he'd asked her along so he could finish explaining what he'd been trying to tell her yesterday, she wouldn't shut him down. But she couldn't imagine it making any difference. Her days at the park were numbered, and she wouldn't be back.

Over lunch he'd told her what Sergei had found at Tenaya Lake. Maybe Ralph and Steve had something to do with the stash of tools, maybe not. Whatever the answer, this was a straightforward case of criminal poaching in a federal park. She was anxious to do her part to help Cal find the criminals responsible.

Little by little they canvassed the area where Ralph and his group had broken off to climb around on their own for an hour.

"We've been going hard," Cal said. "Let's stop for a little while."

He reached inside his backpack for water for both of them. She found a log and sat down to drink hers. In a minute he straddled the end of it.

Alex looked all around. "This place feels enchanted. Did you ever see an old film called *The Enchanted Forest?*"

He was studying her features. "No, but I've heard some of the older tourists talk about it."

"Mom loves films of the '40's. I've watched a lot of them with her. This little boy gets lost and a kind old hermit who made his home in a redwood tree takes care of him until his parents come for him. It really captured my imagination. I used to think how exciting it would be to live in a tree like that."

Alex smiled at the memory.

"When Dad first brought me to the park, we went to see the Giant Sequoias because he knew what it would mean to me. That's when I fell in love with Yosemite. I had my own enchanted forest and my own hermit in Chief Sam Dick."

"Did you tell *him* that story?"

"Yes."

"What did he say to you?"

"He just looked at me for a long time and smiled. You

know the way he does with those eyes of his that seem to see things no one else sees."

"I'm sure you enchanted him. He might not have said it, but you're easy to look at."

Alex laughed at the absurdity of the remark and shook her head.

Cal didn't join in. "He's a man. When you first showed up at the park years ago, every ranger had a comment about Senator Harcourt's gorgeous college-aged daughter. Some things they said would make you blush. How many rangers made a play for you, Alex?"

At the direction of his conversation, her pulse sped up. "You really want to know?" She took another drink of water from her bottle.

"That many," he muttered with a dash of sarcasm when she avoided a reply.

"None of it matters because only one ranger ever caught my attention. He looked, but that was all he did."

The enigmatic male seated near her frowned. "You know why."

Alex poured the last little trickle of water over Sergei's nose and watched him lick it. "You had every right to your reasons. Unfortunately I ignored them year after year. Let's change the subject, shall we?"

"Let's not." He threw his leg back over the log and stood up. "After what Helen did to my brother, I was scared. Because Jack and I were so much alike, I figured it was just a matter of time before I met a woman who would get a stranglehold on me. Once I'd started work in Idaho, I had relationships with women when I was in the mood. I just made certain the ones I chose could be enjoyed for the moment. Safe."

Alex cast him a frank glance. "You mean forgettable."

"For want of a better word, yes. After I became a ranger, I was assigned to work at Rocky National Park, where I met Leeann. She was my age and loved being a ranger. We had good times together. If I hadn't been transferred so soon, we probably would have married and still be there."

"Why didn't you make it work anyway?"

"She wanted to, but I wasn't ready yet. I needed to get a career going first. We stayed in touch, but I was much too taken with Yosemite to have marriage on my mind. Then I met you."

His eyes bored into hers. "Vance saw my reaction to you and said, 'Alex Harcourt is like one of Yosemite's wonders, but she's the senator's pride and joy. The Park needs him on our side, so enjoy the sight, but poach at your peril and mine.'"

Her breath caught. "He actually said that?"

"As God is my witness. It shocked me that I could be that attracted to someone so much younger. You know the rest. I believed all the reasons why I shouldn't be interested in you. Eventually Leeann got transferred to Yosemite and we took up where we left off."

"By now you were ready for marriage."

He nodded. "I loved her in my own way and the timing was right, but a long life together wasn't in our future to be. I meant it when I said I'd like us to start over. I never gave us a chance before. Will you at least consider it before you toss something away that could be vital for both of us?"

WITH HIS QUESTION HANGING in the air, Cal gathered the empty water bottles and put them in his backpack before they started hiking back down to the parking area. Even if she couldn't answer him yet, this day wasn't over, not by a long shot.

Alex moved like the wind, and the dog was only too happy to track her. The ground they'd taken several hours to crisscross was covered in half the time going back. She'd passed the dam and was headed for the campground where they'd parked their vehicles. Cal tightened his grip on the leash and started running in order to catch up to her before she reached his car.

Sergei started barking. Cal thought it was because his dog was excited about getting close to Alex. Everything was a game to him. But when he drew closer, he heard bloodcurdling screams. Soon he came across the kind of frozen tableau of terrified campers he'd visualized from the moment he'd decided to get a bear dog.

He counted twenty tourists. All of them had fled the two picnic tables. On the top of one, a good-sized black bear sat chowing down noisily on the food the campers hadn't eaten. Cal's gaze flew to Alex, who was over by his Xterra, within two feet of another mature black bear.

His heart did a triple jump. All it would take was one great swat of his claws for the bear to knock her down and start gnawing on her, but for the moment the animal stood on his hind legs looking into the car. He made grunting sounds while he searched for more food.

Thank heaven Alex knew what to do and didn't move a muscle.

When the bears ran out of food, Cal knew what could happen, but he didn't have to worry. Sergei was tugging on the leash in a fury and trying to reach the bear at the car. He made bone-chilling sounds worse than any coyote, the kind that could damage an eardrum.

He sounded so ferocious, the bear finally got back down on all fours and ran off into the trees. Now that Sergei was in bear-attack mode, Cal was overjoyed to watch him do what he'd been born to do. The hours he'd spent training him had paid off. His dog turned to the picnic table to charge the other bear and harass him.

Everyone stood on the perimeter and watched in fear and fascination as the bear stopped eating, recognizing the barking menace wasn't about to go away. With reluctance, he finally gave up and got down. Sergei let out another volley of savage inhuman sounds, causing the bear to drop the hot dogs in his paws before he turned to follow his cohort into the forest with a roar.

The sight thrilled Cal to the core.

Sergei tried to follow and yanked at the leash, but Cal held him back and got down on his haunches. "Good boy, Sergei! Good job!" He threw his arm around Sergei's neck and gave him some doggie treats. "That's the way to do it, buddy. That's the idea."

Suddenly Alex was there at his other side, hugging the dog for all she was worth and kissing his head. "You saved the day, Sergei." The happiness in her voice rang in the air. "Good dog. You're wonderful! I love you!"

As she lifted tear-filled eyes to Cal, they both heard clapping, but he was hardly aware of the crowd converging around them. The awed look in the green depths of her eyes coupled with her outpouring of words—even if she was caught up in the emotion of the moment—filled him with an elation he'd never known before.

The comments from the campers seemed never ending— "We can never thank you enough," being the most repeated. While he and Sergei became the center of attention and posed for pictures, Alex made her getaway as Cal knew she would. He didn't mind now. After he'd had a talk with the tourists and reassured them the bears wouldn't be back, he planned to head for Yosemite Valley to find her.

DURING THE DRIVE BACK, Alex's legs felt weak as water. Though she'd been coming to the park for years, she'd never been that close to a hungry bear before. Cal had taught her what she should do in case of an incident, but she'd never had to act on his instructions.

What if he hadn't followed her down? What if Sergei hadn't been with them? Like everyone at the picnic tables, she'd been taken by complete surprise when the bears showed up out of the blue. She was shaking so hard in reaction, she needed to talk to someone about it. Without conscious thought she reached for her cell and phoned Chief Rossiter.

He answered on the fourth ring. "Alex? It's good to hear your voice. What's up, my favorite sleuth?" he teased.

"Vance? I'm so glad you answered!"

"Are you in trouble?"

"No, no. Actually things couldn't be better," she said

in a shaky voice. "You told me to report to you when I noted something good or bad happening around the park. Well, this afternoon I have something phenomenal to report. Since I know Cal will play it down like it was nothing, I wanted you to know that he and Sergei came to the rescue today in a huge way. I wouldn't be surprised if the tourists involved don't spread it around the park."

"Go on."

She got straight to the point, leaving nothing out except of a personal nature. "You should have seen how grateful those campers were. They had a couple of children with them. The dog got rid of the bears like magic. I've never seen anything like it in my life."

"Yeah?" She felt Vance's excitement through the phone.

"His bark terrified *me!*"

Vance gave a hearty laugh.

"Cal deserves some kind of recognition for what he did." Her voice cracked as she said it.

"I couldn't agree more."

"If other rangers could train more bear dogs who'd behave like Sergei, you could turn the bear problem around in the park. I wish I had a video to show you."

"So do I."

"Vance? Would you consider letting the Trent Foundation set up a fund for more dogs?" There was a protracted silence. "You don't have to answer me now. I realize you'd have to pick rangers who'd be willing to work with an animal all the time. Maybe there aren't that many who'd be committed. But if Cal trained them…"

She was running off at the mouth. That's what a close shave with a terrifying bear encounter had done to her.

"Just think about it, but don't tell Cal. I don't want him to know I shared this with you. He's so modest he'll just blow off what happened this afternoon anyway. Let him think it came from someone else."

"I hear you. Tell me—while you were out, did you come across any other stashes of weapons or mutilations?"

"We combed the area for a long time, but unless Cal noticed something I didn't, then no. He's still at the campground. I'm on my way back to the ski lodge. I need to check in with the guys."

"Understood. We'll keep in touch. And Alex—I'm thankful you all came out of today's adventure safe."

Her lungs took an extra breath. "So am I. Talk to you later." She hung up feeling a little less shaken until she phoned Lonan and found out he was at the clinic with Lokita.

"It's his appendix."

"He had a bout with that last year," Alex said.

"That explains why he hasn't felt good the last couple of days. The doctor says it needs to come out, but he's fighting me on it."

"He has to have the operation. Where are the boys?"

"Swimming at the Yosemite Lodge."

"I'll be there shortly. Do you want to drive him to the hospital in Merced, or shall I?"

"He's refusing to go anywhere, Alex."

If Lonan couldn't budge him, then Lokita was being his most stubborn self. "I'll be at the clinic shortly."

After they hung up, Alex phoned Cal. She had to get his permission. It was his car she was driving after all.

"Alex?" He sounded upset. "Why haven't you picked up? I've been trying to reach you."

"I'm sorry. I…was on the phone with Lonan."

She heard a sharp intake of breath. "After that scare, you shouldn't have gone off alone. I can tell something's wrong. What is it?"

When she told him he said, "I'm five minutes behind you and will meet you at the clinic. Just keep your phone line open!"

"I will," she said, secretly relieved and surprised he was so close. *And thrilled.* Before another moment passed she needed to call Lokita's parents and tell them what was happening. They were the only ones who could get him to see reason.

Or so she thought.

When she arrived a half hour later, she found him sitting in the reception room next to Lonan, shaking his dark head. He refused to look up at Alex.

She and Lonan exchanged a concerned glance before she whispered she'd take over. Lonan looked relieved and wished her luck before he left the clinic to round up the other teens.

Alex stood in front of him. "Did you talk to your parents?"

"Yes."

"Did they tell you to go to the hospital?"

"Yes. I said no."

"Are you trying to prove how brave you are?"

His mouth tightened.

"You'll show the guys what brave is if you go. They hate the idea of a hospital. Everyone does."

"Alex is right" came a deep, familiar voice behind

her. She felt it resonate clear through her. Cal's presence brought Lokita's head up. He sat down next to the boy. No doubt Cal had bumped into Lonan and knew what was wrong. The boys had certain apprehensions about Western medicine.

"I had my appendix out at your age."

"You?" the teen questioned in surprise.

"Yup. It was over so fast, I got to go back home the same day. If you want to see my scar, I'll show it to you. It's tiny, but I always considered it my mark of bravery."

Lokita looked Cal up and down. "Will you come with me?"

The smile Cal gave the teen would stay with Alex all her life. "I wouldn't be anywhere else. Neither would Alex. We'll keep you company."

"Okay."

Thank heaven for Cal. He'd won the boys' trust. There could be no greater compliment.

The teen stood up slowly. He was in pain. "Let's go."

They left the clinic. While Cal put Lokita in the back-seat of the car, Alex climbed in front. Cal came around the other side and started the car.

"Where's Sergei?"

"I dropped him off at Jeff's for the night."

For the night. Alex's heart raced at the thought, but right now Lokita was their first priority.

To keep Lokita's thoughts off himself during the drive to Merced, she told him all about the bear incident at the Hetch Hetchy in great detail. "You should have seen

Sergei scare those bears away with that savage bark. You would have loved it."

"Lokita?" Cal interjected. "Did I ever tell you guys a bear can run thirty miles an hour? Well, I figure I could have clocked them going forty."

Alex laughed hard, still picturing the bear dropping the hot dogs before he hightailed it out of there. "That's our Sergei."

The words flew out of her mouth before she realized what she'd said. Her gaze collided with Cal's. What she read in that look electrified her just as it had the first time they'd met.

Chapter Eleven

Alex could feel something tickling her nose. She lifted her hand and encountered another hand. Her eyes fluttered open. Early-morning light was coming through the shutters of the hospital room window. The next thing she knew Cal's lips smothered her little cry.

"Shh… You'll waken Lokita. We have to whisper."

It took a minute for her to realize Cal had moved his cot next to hers. Last night after Lokita had been brought back from a successful laparoscopic appendectomy, housekeeping had placed Cal's cot on the other side of the hospital bed.

"All I ask is that you listen," he implored her.

That was all she *could* do while her heart was thundering in every pulse point of her body. When he spoke, his whiskers tickled her skin. She loved the feel of them. She loved every single thing about him.

"While I've got you where I want you, there's something you need to know. When I was kissing you at the lookout tower, I knew deep in my gut I wanted you in my life, but because of all the reasons we've talked about, I didn't act on my feelings at the time to keep you there."

"Cal—"

"I swear it's true." His voice trembled slightly. "When I bumped into you outside the Chief's office, I couldn't prevent myself from going after you. Say you believe me." He spoke with an earnestness she'd never heard before. "I love you, Alex. I've been desperately in love with you for a long, long time."

When she opened her mouth to speak, he held up a hand. "After you came to the park with your father the first time, I knew in my gut I'd met someone I'd never forget. The night at the Ahwahnee when you were seated at the dining room table with your boys, everyone could see your great love for them. It was there in your eyes... your sweetness and goodness. Your generosity. Right then I realized I would sell my soul if I could get you to love *me* like that."

It seemed like she'd been waiting an eternity to hear those words.

"I do love you like that, Cal." It was heaven to be able to finally admit it to him. "I've been in love with you forever, but then you've always known that."

Too filled with her love for him to talk anymore, she slid her arm around his neck and pulled him closer so she could show him what he meant to her. The joy of knowing he welcomed her kiss was so liberating, she had no inhibitions. What started out as one kiss grew into another until there was no beginning, no end.

"This is torture," he whispered into her silky hair sometime later. His breathing sounded ragged. "If I make one more move, both our cots will collapse, but it's killing me not to be able to do what I want to you."

"That works both ways," she whispered back, loving the feel of his hair while she ran her hands through it.

"You shouldn't have told me that. When the doctor releases Lokita, we'll take him to my house to recover for another couple of days. In between nursing him, we'll have our privacy. How does that sound?" His compelling mouth was already covering hers again.

"You already know" were the only words she could manage before their hunger took over. The driving force of his kiss broke down the barriers between them, robbing her of strength. She clung to him and found herself responding with a ferocity she couldn't control.

Alex had never experienced anything that came anywhere near this divine, wild ecstasy permeating her heart and body. She loved Cal to the depth of her being and couldn't prevent herself from showing him. Neither of them was aware of anything until they heard footsteps outside the door.

At the sound she started to come to her senses and tried to break off their kiss, but Cal moaned his displeasure and held her trapped in his strong arms. When the door opened, she pushed against his chest, forcing him to relinquish his hold.

Embarrassed, she tore swollen lips from his. Cal's hands slid reluctantly from her, finally allowing her to roll away from him.

"Don't mind *me*," the nurse said drily as she walked over to check on Lokita. "The doctor's making rounds now. He ought to be here in a minute."

Red-faced, Alex got to her feet on legs of mush and headed for the bathroom to freshen up. She had to cling to the sink until the room stopped spinning. When she came out, she discovered the cots were gone.

The middle-aged surgeon stood at the foot of the bed talking to Cal. It wasn't fair for a man who'd lost sleep for the past two nights doing park business to look so incredibly attractive.

"Lokita's coming along fine," the doctor said to her. "So far no complications in twelve hours. He's anxious to go home, so I see no reason why he can't leave by noon. The nurse will give you a set of instructions to take with you." He patted the teenager on the shoulder. "You'll be up and around in a few days, son, good as new."

"Thanks," Lokita murmured.

"You're welcome."

Cal walked the doctor out to the hall. Alex moved over to the side of the bed. "How are you feeling right now?" she asked Lokita.

"Strange."

"I'm very proud of you."

He looked embarrassed. "Cal says I can stay at his house tonight. Is that okay?"

"Yes. I'm going to be there with you."

"Can the guys come and see me?"

"Absolutely. In fact we'll have a party tonight after they get back from work." He gave her the first smile she'd seen from him in days. "But right now you need to sleep until it's time to go. Do you want to say hi to your parents first?"

"Yes."

She got them on the phone and handed it to Lokita before she slipped out the door. There was no sign of Cal, who'd probably gone to bring them coffee. She couldn't bear for him to be out of her sight, not for a single second.

He loved her.

The magic of that word…

CAL LOOKED AROUND HIS living room filled with teenagers. Never in his wildest dreams could he have imagined such a scenario when he'd moved in here in mid-May.

Except for Lonan, who sat on the easy chair, the rest had plopped on the floor around the couch where Lokita was lying while they ate ice-cream sundaes, Alex's idea. It was a huge hit. Cal had already eaten his fill and had just scarfed his third brownie.

Alex came in and out of the kitchen, her face flushed making sure everyone got enough to eat. Though he had to keep his hands off her, Cal couldn't prevent himself from kissing her soundly each time. This was joy as he'd never experienced it.

During the party, Jeff arrived with Sergei. The presence of the dog raised the level of celebration several notches higher. He dived for Alex, proof he'd bonded with her, too. Afterward he came to find Cal before the boys coaxed him to play.

"Come on in the kitchen, Jeff."

He followed Cal. Alex brought up the rear. "What kind of toppings do you want on your sundae, Ranger Thompson?"

He lounged in one of the chairs, grinning up at her. "The works."

Cal no longer had to imagine Alex in his house. She

was here for real and wouldn't be going anywhere again. Not without him.

"Here you go. Take a brownie, too."

"Thanks. I could get used to this kind of attention."

She flashed both men a heart-stopping smile before leaving the kitchen with more treats for the guys. Cal straddled the other chair, still pinching himself that this miracle had really happened. For a minute neither of them said anything. Jeff just continued to stare at him.

"You know who you resemble, don't you?"

"I haven't a clue."

He ate most of his ice cream before he said, "You've got a dopey grin on your face just like the Chief's after Parker was born. Like you're so happy you don't know where to go with it."

"Is that a fact."

"You know it is. I take it something profound happened to you over the last two days and the woman in the other room is the reason."

Cal was too insane with excitement to do anything more than nod.

"When's the wedding?"

"First I have to get her alone to ask her. Much as I'd like to move her in with me tonight, I can't. Don't ask me why."

Jeff chuckled. "That's what you get for living in a goldfish bowl."

The only flaw to their private community. "Thanks for taking care of Sergei."

"Hey—he and I had a great time. I might get me one."

"Too bad there's no funding."

"Oh, but there is."

"Since when?"

"Since Sergei sniffed out that cache of weapons. *And*, more recently, since some tourists came by headquarters yesterday and told Vance how Sergei got rid of those bears at the campground."

This was news to Cal.

"It's the talk of the park. You and your dog are famous. Vance says this will open up some funding to pay for a full program."

Cal shot to his feet. "You're kidding me—"

"Nope. Not about this. He's even talking about you doing the training. Now for the bad news. He wants us over at headquarters, stat."

"No way." Not with Alex under his roof at last.

"Afraid so. There's a new development in the case. Go tell her and get it over with."

"ALEX?" LOKITA WHISPERED. "Is it really okay for me to sleep in Cal's bed?"

"Of course. And you don't need to whisper because everyone has gone." She made sure he took his antibiotic, then drew the covers over him. "We both want you to get well in a hurry. You need a lot of rest where you'll be comfortable. Are you in pain?"

He shook his head. "You love him."

A simple statement that said everything. She sank down on the side of the mattress and smiled at him. "Yes. So much."

"He's a good man."

Her eyes filled with tears. Coming from one of her

young Zuni friends, those honest words meant more to her than anything in the world.

"Lokita? Tell me something before I turn out the light. Do you think I made a mistake bringing you boys here?"

He frowned. "Who said that?"

"No one. But I worry. Maybe you all came because I wanted you to, and now you wish you could go home but you're afraid to tell me."

"That's funny."

She blinked. "Why do you say that?"

"We're afraid you'll take us back."

"Why would I do that?"

"Because some of the other volunteers don't like us."

"Then they're the ones who need to go home. Haven't you made friends with Andy?"

"Yes."

"You see? You heard Cal. Some people will never change their views, but that's not everyone."

Alex saw the relief in his dark eyes. "We've already voted to stay the whole time, but we haven't told Halian yet."

Her heart had run out of places to expand. "Thank you for telling me that. Now it's time to go to sleep. Sergei would like to stay in here with you." The dog lay right by the bed. "Is that okay?"

"I want him to."

She knew that. "If you need anything, just call out."

"I'm fine."

"You heard Cal. If you get hungry, help yourself to

anything in the kitchen. We bought you Popsicle treats and Cap'n Crunch cereal, your favorite."

"Thanks."

"Good night, Lokita. Sleep well."

Alex switched off the light and went into the kitchen to clean up. As soon as the dishes were done, she started in on the living room. Anything to keep busy until Cal came back. She knew how long those meetings could go.

With nothing more to be done, she finally lay down on the couch and pulled the blanket over her. It was an extra one Cal had gotten out of the linen cupboard for Lokita. She was exhausted, but there was one difference between tonight and all the other nights since she'd known Ranger Hollis.

He wanted her here when he got back. He'd given her orders before he'd left the house with Jeff.

She'd heard a little residual fear in his voice and understood it because she couldn't quite believe he was really hers until he returned and held her again.

Alex didn't remember when she fell asleep, but the next time she was aware of her surroundings, it was morning. She came awake suddenly and sat up to discover Cal in a sleeping bag on the floor next to her, out like a light. He'd thrown the top part off him at some point during the night, probably because he'd gotten too hot.

Delight filled her. Only one other time had she seen him in navy sweats like the ones he was wearing now. That was when she'd surprised him in his tent, one of her more foolish escapades. But she wouldn't dwell on that now. It was time to focus on the present.

She turned over on her stomach and crept close to the edge of the couch so she could look at him. He lay on his side facing her, one arm beneath his head, the other outstretched. His disheveled dark blond hair and five o'clock shadow only added to his rugged masculinity. She took in the long, hard-muscled length of him. Was he the most beautiful man in existence or what?

As she was studying each feature, his eyes opened. They glowed like blue suns. She stared into them for a long time while the two of them communed in breathtaking silence. It had been a painful journey to this point for both of them, but Alex could never doubt the love she saw there now. She was the first to break the quiet.

"I love you."

"Marry me?" he asked in a voice an octave deeper than usual.

She smiled. "I thought you'd never ask."

He raised himself up on one elbow. "How would you like Chief Sam Dick to do the honors? He has the authority here in the park. We could have a small ceremony among the Sequoias with our families and the boys. I can't promise to set us up in a tree to live. I'm afraid this house will have to do, but when our children come along, they can play among the big trees and dream the way you did."

"Cal—"

"Is that a yes?" He still sounded anxious.

"You know it is. I love you more than life itself."

"I don't see how. I treated you horribly. Alex—"

"No more explanations are necessary." She sat up. "No more saying we're sorry to each other. I understand about Leeann. I understand it all. My parents worried about me coming back to the park again. I understood that, too, but it was something I had to do.

"I've been given more opportunities than most people could ever dream of and I wanted to share them with these boys, who never knew their birth parents. They weren't given the great start in life I was. I also wanted to prove to you that I could handle being rejected by you with grace. If I couldn't have you, I at least wanted to leave a better impression than I did when you first met me."

"You impressed me years ago. I knew your love for the park was genuine and realized we were kindred spirits in many ways. I fell hard for you, Alex, but too many things got in the way."

"That's the difference between men and women. Once a woman sees what she wants, that's it."

"Then why aren't you down here with me?"

"Because I need to thank you for what you've done first, and I can't talk when I'm that close to you." In a rush of words she told him about her conversation with Lokita. "You're the one who turned this whole experience around for the boys. Last night you brought them into your home, made them feel important."

"Because they *are,*" he declared. "While Jeff was in the kitchen with me, he told me Vance wants to honor Lusio and Mika. Telford's hoping you'll let him do a press release with pictures. I have to admit this is the kind of publicity the park could use."

She smiled. "The boys would love it."

"Because of them the case has been solved."

"Solved?"

"You'll be interested to know forensics dusted for

fingerprints from Ralph and Brock's rooms when they weren't around. They matched the ones lifted off the knives and chisels. Last evening they were arrested."

"So Brock was in on it, too. I can't say I'm completely surprised."

"Vance says your instincts are dead on, and he's right. DNA samples have been taken. My hunch is, theirs will match up with the ones taken at the bear mutilation site last year. If so, those two will go to prison for a long time."

"Good. The picture of those poor, torn-up animals will always be in my memory. What about Steve?"

"He was taken into custody, too. The investigators found out he has access to drugs through his mom, who's a pharmacist. Steve was one of the at-risk students Ralph Thorn had been working with at the school.

"I understand his father abandoned him. In exchange for tranquilizers, Thorn probably promised him a share of the take. We don't know how deeply he's involved yet. That will be for the court to decide."

He took a deep breath. "Are we through talking now, darling? There are other things I want to do and can't wait any longer."

"Just give me thirty seconds to text my mom."

He checked his watch. "I'm counting."

She reached for her phone on the end table and pressed the digits. When she'd finished, she slid to the floor and wrapped her arms around him, relishing the feel of him.

"That had to be the shortest message on record. What did you say to her?"

"Here." She clicked the button so he could read what she'd sent.

"*The best woman won'?*"

Alex nodded before pushing the phone away. "She'll know what I mean. Before I flew to Yosemite for the volunteer interview she hugged me and said, 'May the best woman win.' It was her way of telling me I was no longer a girl and she was rooting for me and my experiment.

"The message I sent back was my way of letting her know I've never been happier in my life, which says it all. Now kiss me and don't stop. Once Lokita's awake, Sergei will come bounding in here and want to play."

"He'll have to wait," Cal said a little testily before he rolled her on her back, on fire for this remarkable, exquisite woman whose mouth and body were telling him she was undeniably his.

* * * * *

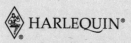
HARLEQUIN®

American ★ Romance®

COMING NEXT MONTH

Available February 8, 2011

#1341 ROUGHNECK COWBOY
American Romance's Men of the West
Marin Thomas

#1342 THE RANCHER'S TWIN TROUBLES
The Buckhorn Ranch
Laura Marie Altom

#1343 HIS VALENTINE SURPRISE
Fatherhood
Tanya Michaels

#1344 OFFICER DADDY
Safe Harbor Medical
Jacqueline Diamond

REQUEST YOUR FREE BOOKS!
2 FREE NOVELS PLUS 2 FREE GIFTS!

HARLEQUIN®

American ★ Romance®

Love, Home & Happiness!

YES! Please send me 2 FREE Harlequin® American Romance® novels and my 2 FREE gifts (gifts are worth about $10). After receiving them, if I don't wish to receive any more books, I can return the shipping statement marked "cancel." If I don't cancel, I will receive 4 brand-new novels every month and be billed just $4.24 per book in the U.S. or $4.99 per book in Canada. That's a saving of at least 15% off the cover price! It's quite a bargain! Shipping and handling is just 50¢ per book.* I understand that accepting the 2 free books and gifts places me under no obligation to buy anything. I can always return a shipment and cancel at any time. Even if I never buy another book from Harlequin, the two free books and gifts are mine to keep forever.

154/354 HDN E5LG

Name _____ (PLEASE PRINT)

Address _____ Apt. #

City _____ State/Prov. _____ Zip/Postal Code

Signature (if under 18, a parent or guardian must sign)

Mail to the Harlequin Reader Service:
IN U.S.A.: P.O. Box 1867, Buffalo, NY 14240-1867
IN CANADA: P.O. Box 609, Fort Erie, Ontario L2A 5X3

Not valid for current subscribers to Harlequin® American Romance® books.

Want to try two free books from another line?
Call 1-800-873-8635 or visit www.morefreebooks.com.

* Terms and prices subject to change without notice. Prices do not include applicable taxes. N.Y. residents add applicable sales tax. Canadian residents will be charged applicable provincial taxes and GST. Offer not valid in Quebec. This offer is limited to one order per household. All orders subject to approval. Credit or debit balances in a customer's account(s) may be offset by any other outstanding balance owed by or to the customer. Please allow 4 to 6 weeks for delivery. Offer available while quantities last.

Your Privacy: Harlequin is committed to protecting your privacy. Our Privacy Policy is available online at www.eHarlequin.com or upon request from the Reader Service. From time to time we make our lists of customers available to reputable third parties who may have a product or service of interest to you. If you would prefer we not share your name and address, please check here. ☐

Help us get it right—We strive for accurate, respectful and relevant communications. To clarify or modify your communication preferences, visit us at www.ReaderService.com/consumerschoice.

HAR10R

*Harlequin Romance author Donna Alward is loved
for her gorgeous rancher heroes.*

*Meet Wyatt as he's confronted by both a precious
little pink bundle left on his doorstep and his neighbor Elli
who's going to show him the ropes....*

Introducing
PROUD RANCHER, PRECIOUS BUNDLE

THE SQUAWKING QUIETED as Elli picked the baby up, and
Wyatt turned around, trying hard to ignore the feelings of
inadequacy as Darcy immediately stopped fussing.

"Maybe she's uncomfortable. What do you think, sweet-
heart?" Elli turned her conversation to the baby.

"What do you think is wrong?" Wyatt asked, putting the
coffee pot back on the burner.

A strange look passed over Elli's face, one that looked
like guilt and panic. But it was gone quickly. "I couldn't
say," she replied.

"But you were so good with her this afternoon." Wyatt
put his hands on his hips.

"Lucky, that's all. I just…remembered a few things."
The same strange look flitted over her features once more.

Wyatt took the coffee to the table. "You fooled me. You
looked like you knew exactly what you were doing." So
much so that Wyatt had felt completely inept. A feeling he
despised. He was used to being the one in control.

Elli and Darcy walked the length of the kitchen and
back. After a few moments, she admitted, "I haven't really
cared for a baby before. The things I thought of were simply
things I'd heard about. Not from experience, Mr. Black."

Her chin jutted up, closing the subject but making him

want to ask the questions now pulsing through his mind. But then he remembered the old saying—*Don't look a gift horse in the mouth.* He'd benefit from whatever insight she had and be glad of it.

"I don't really know what babies need," he said. "I fed her, patted her back like you did, walked her to sleep, but every time I put her down…"

Wyatt almost groaned. Of course. He'd forgotten one important thing. He'd been so focused on getting the formula the right temperature that he'd forgotten to check her diaper. Not that he had any clue what to do there either.

Pulling calves and shoveling out stalls was far less intimidating than one tiny newborn.

"She's probably due for a diaper change, isn't she." He tried to sound nonchalant. This was a perfect opportunity. Elli must know how to change a diaper. He could simply watch her so he'd know better for the next time.

Instead, Elli came around the corner of the counter and placed Darcy back in his arms. "Here you go, Uncle Wyatt," she said lightly. "You get diaper duty. I'll fix the coffee. Cream and sugar?"

Oh boy, Wyatt thought, looking down into Darcy's pursed face, his smug plan blown to smithereens. He was in for it now.

Will sparks fly between Elli and Wyatt?

Find out in
PROUD RANCHER, PRECIOUS BUNDLE
Available February 2011 from Harlequin Romance

Try these Healthy and Delicious Spring Rolls!

INGREDIENTS

2 packages rice-paper
spring roll wrappers
(20 wrappers)

1 cup grated carrot

¼ cup bean sprouts

1 cucumber, julienned

1 red bell pepper, without
stem and seeds, julienned

4 green onions
finely chopped—
use only the green part

DIRECTIONS

1. Soak one rice-paper wrapper
   in a large bowl of hot water
   until softened.

2. Place a pinch each of carrots,
   sprouts, cucumber, bell
   pepper and green onion on the
   wrapper toward the bottom
   third of the rice paper.

3. Fold ends in and roll tightly
   to enclose filling.

4. Repeat with remaining
   wrappers. Chill before
   serving.

Find this and many more delectable recipes
including the perfect dipping sauce in

NTRSERIESJAN